Strange Relations

by Sonia Levitin

LAUREL-LEAF BOOKS

My heartfelt thanks to Charna and Chaim Mentz, of Chabad of Bel Air, for countless hours of
teaching and gracious hospitality and for bringing me to *Yiddishkeit* and the love of tradition.

Thanks to Pearl Krasnjansky of Chabad of Hawaii, for her inspiration and encouragement
and for being a model *aishes chayil*, "woman of valor."

Thanks to my dear friend Miriam Wiener for generously sharing her story.

Thanks to Mardi Goldman, a vital member of the local *Chevra Kadisha*, the Jewish Burial Society,
for information about this important ritual.

For Lloyd, husband, hero, friend
With love

Published by Laurel-Leaf, an imprint of Random House Children's Books,
a division of Random House, Inc. New York

This is a work of fiction. Names, characters, places, and incidents either are the product of the author's imagination
or are used fictitiously. Any resemblance to actual persons, living or dead, events, or locales is entirely coincidental.

Originally published in hardcover in the United States by Alfred A. Knopf Books for Young Readers,
New York, in 2007. This edition published by arrangement with Alfred A. Knopf Books for Young Readers.

Laurel-Leaf and colophon are registered trademarks of Random House, Inc.

Visit us on the Web! www.randomhouse.com/teens

Educators and librarians, for a variety of teaching tools, visit us at www.randomhouse.com/teachers

The Library of Congress has cataloged the hardcover edition of this work as follows:
Levitin, Sonia.
Strange relations / Sonia Levitin.
p. cm.
Summary: Fifteen-year-old Marne is excited to be able to spend her summer vacation in Hawaii,
not realizing the change in her lifestyle it would bring staying with her aunt,
seven cousins, and uncle who is a Chasidic rabbi.
ISBN: 978-0-375-83751-7 (trade)—ISBN: 978-0-375-93751-4 (lib. bdg.)
1. Jews—Hawaii—Juvenile fiction. [1. Jews—United States—Fiction. 2. Hawaii—Fiction.
3. Cousins—Fiction. 4. Religion—Fiction. 5. Friendship—Fiction.] I. Title.
PZ7.L58St 2007
[Fic]—dc22
2006033275

ISBN: 978-0-440-23963-5 (pbk.)
RL: 7.0
April 2009
Printed in the United States of America
10 9 8 7 6 5 4 3 2 1
First Laurel-Leaf Edition

Marne used to hear the hum of their voices through the wall separating their bedrooms. Late at night, when her father came home from the hospital, she'd awaken to hear them murmuring and laughing. It sounded gentle and soft, like the ocean waves in the distance.

Now there was only silence, punctuated by short phrases dropped like pebbles onto wood. They were not angry, only brief. A tiredness lodged in her parents' voices, and it showed in their eyes, too, as if they were thinking of other times, other places. Marne remembered how on Saturday mornings they all used to sit together on the huge sectional sofa, that soft, downy monster, leaning into one another and laughing at some cartoon on TV. When they got hungry, they'd dash into the kitchen, and Mom would make pancakes. They ate stacks of pancakes covered with Mom's special raspberry syrup.

Later Mom made another of her snappy decisions. "Too fattening." So now even for Sunday breakfast they shook dry cereal into their bowls, unless Dad went out and brought back bagels and cream cheese and lox. Marne would open the package with the smoked salmon, which glistened on the smooth waxy paper. Dad would slice an onion very thin, then settle down to engross himself in the *Times*. Mom would sit by the window with her sketch pad, drawing lean, long-legged women wearing astonishing combinations of denim and silk, with dazzling beadwork and touches of original print. "Innovative designer," her CEO called her. "Purely out of the box." Her mom was clever with her hands. Marne remembered how they used to hang out at the beach, making sand people and watching Dad get into his wet suit and hit the surf. The surfer kids called him an old-timer and wondered when he'd ever quit. "When I'm six feet under," he'd say. "Out on that ocean, you forget everything but the wave."

There was a quiet moment, like a truce, then perfunctory conversation. "Will you be home for dinner tomorrow?"

"No. We're one person short at the pharmacy."

"Well, then Marne and I will go out for something."

They would walk over to the Mariner's for fresh crab and French bread. Her mom had a glass of wine, only one.

"I don't like to lose control," she'd say. While they watched the waves, Mom would ask Marne about school, considering it "quality time."

Their voices rose again. Marne, hunched over her math papers, tried to fix her mind on the equations, but the voices intruded.

"What do you suggest, then?" There was that edge in her mother's voice, like paper being ripped.

"Send her to camp."

"She's fifteen years old. You don't just send . . ."

"There must be some camp for kids like her."

"What do you mean, like her?"

"Hey, lay off me! I mean where they have sports, put on plays."

"She hated that Scout camp."

"Can't she stay with a friend? What about Kim?"

"They're traveling . . . can't impose . . ."

"Then take her with you."

"To Paris? Are you nuts?"

Silence held for a minute or two. Marne sat, clutching her pencil, unable to focus.

Words exploded. "Your parents . . ."

"Busy . . . why should they?"

"So damned selfish! Never bothered . . ."

"They're entitled . . ."

"Hire a companion . . ."

"Like who?"

Marne jumped up, shoved her books aside, and hurried out into the hall. She stood at their door, waiting for her breath to even out. If she burst in, all in a frenzy, they wouldn't be able to handle it.

Marne stood at their door, gaining control, formulating the right words. She had been holding the idea in her mind since yesterday morning, when at dawn she went out for her run on the boardwalk. As she ran, the deep darkness that closed off the edge of the sky began to lift, quite as if a lid had been pulled up from the earth by a gigantic hand. Suddenly, where there had been only inky blackness, light emerged, and then the sky was filled with exquisite colors of orange, lavender, and rose. In that moment the idea struck her. *Hawaii. Aunt Carole. Hawaii for the summer. Why not?* She'd make it happen.

Kim and her family were going to Hawaii in July. "I wish you could go with us," Kim had said, showing Marne the wraparound skirts and sandals she and her three sisters bought for their vacation in paradise. That was what the brochures said, showing broad, sandy beaches and umbrella-like trees covered with blossoms.

"Don't I wish it, too," Marne had said longingly. She immediately regretted her tone—too needy. "I love your family," she added, trying to sound nonchalant. She did love being with them. Just spending the night at Kim's was cool. Someone was always singing or yelling, dancing to a CD, fixing guacamole or chocolate chip cookies, doing things to their hair or having a facial.

As she ran toward the sunrise and back again toward home, Marne worked out the details. She could get an inexpensive flight. She'd already be there when Kim arrived. They could spend time together at the beach. Maybe Kim's folks would include her in some activities. They'd probably have rented a whole condo for the gang. Meanwhile, she'd do errands for Aunt Carole, help her with the kids. It sounded odd, *Aunt Carole*. Marne had seen her aunt only twice in her life; the last time was five years ago. Then, nothing really stuck. It was like a dream, a cacophony of voices and faces and too many questions. All she remembered from that time was seeing Carole at the kitchen stove, stirring a huge pot with chicken and vegetables and spices.

What little Marne knew about her aunt Carole came from Mom's snappy words, and the way she rolled her eyes and tucked in her lips when she spoke of her sister. "Over the top, she is. Don't know exactly what made her that way. Nobody else in our family ever got so peculiar. Well, to each his own."

Every year or two they'd get a birth announcement. Mom would smirk and say, "It's from Carole. Another baby. I don't know how she does it."

"The usual way, I'll bet," Dad would say.

"She's a regular rabbit. God! Can you imagine, she's got five already. Well, to each his own."

Marne knocked once, then again, louder. The voices ceased.

"I've got a solution," Marne said as she walked into the room. She made herself grin, lighten up. It was the only way to deal with them. "This is it. You'll love it. Send me to Hawaii. Aunt Carole's got so many kids she won't even notice an extra body."

They both turned to stare at her. Marne could see her mother thinking, formulating objections. She always said no at first.

"It's out of the question," she finally said. "You couldn't stand it. I couldn't stand it for even a week."

"It might be a learning experience," said Marne, feeling sly.

"Why would Carole want you?"

"I could help her with the baby. I'm good with babies."

"I haven't talked to Carole in ages," Mom said. Her arms were crossed over her chest. "I'm not even sure what island she's on."

"How do you know she has room for you?" Dad asked.

"I could sleep on the floor. I'm a good sleeper."

"How would you get there?" her mother asked.

"I guess I could walk," Marne said, and laughed. Her dad chuckled.

"It's an idea, Nance," he said.

"You mean, the whole summer?" Mom asked.

"We could still talk on the phone," Marne said. "I'd call you every week. Both of you. You could relax. I'd be having fun."

"My sister isn't exactly a fun person," her mother said. She began to fold things—panty hose, a sweater, a towel. "I suppose I could pay Carole something. I don't think they have much money, she and Itch."

"Itch? Is that his name?"

"Something like that."

"Does he make people itch?" Marne quipped.

"Cut it out," said her mother crossly. "Whatever gave you such an idea? Look, these are peculiar people. She may be my sister, but she's . . ."

"They aren't dangerous, Nance," her father said. "They're family, after all."

"So they're a little strange," Marne said. "Strange relations," she mused.

"Relatives," her mother snapped, still sounding testy.

"*Relations* is better," her father interjected, grinning. He put his hand on the top of Marne's head. "You know, as in *relationship*."

"Well, we certainly don't have much of a relationship with Carole," Mom said. She sighed. "I can already tell, you two are conspiring. Strange relations, indeed," she said, but a slight smile played around her lips.

Marne said, "Maybe I could email her. Do you think she has email?"

"I told you, I don't know what she has, Marne. I haven't talked to Carole since—last year when the baby was born, I sent the cutest little outfit from the Gap. Carole never even called to thank me. Just sent a card with a scribble."

"I could phone her."

"I don't even know where I kept her phone number."

"It's in the box," Marne said. "The clutter box."

Mom threw up her hands. "Look, I think this is a wild-goose chase. I don't think you realize that Carole's lifestyle is highly . . . well . . . unusual."

"So? You're always saying it takes all kinds."

"I'll bet she doesn't have room or time for a house-guest."

"So, if she says I can come, it's okay?"

Her parents looked at each other, and for a moment Marne felt as in the old days, before everything shattered. "Maybe I could get a week off, Nance," her father said softly. "I could meet you in Paris."

"Oh, Harry," said her mother.

"Go and call," said her father. "It's three hours earlier there. They'll still be up."

"I don't think Carole ever sleeps," said her mother. "Overachiever."

"Look who's talking," said her dad. He pointed at Mom. "Going to Paris to work with that chichi designer all summer. What did Pierre say about you?"

Mom smiled slightly and waved him away. "Forget it. It's all hype."

"We could go to the Louvre," her father said. "The Tuileries. Remember?"

"I'll be working, Harry. This is not a pleasure trip."

"Well, I only thought . . ."

"You're always hinting about going to Costa Rica to surf. Why don't you do it?"

Marne ran upstairs to get Aunt Carole's telephone number. The house was inverted, bedrooms below. The living room upstairs offered a slight view of the ocean. It was the reason they had bought this house, with its three tiny bedrooms, too small, really, but rustic and satisfying, with the sound of the sea and the fresh salt air.

After what neighbors and acquaintances called "the incident," they might have moved, but every time the idea came up, it was immediately discarded. "No. What if they are trying to locate us? No. We can't leave."

On the mantel stood the redwood box, filled with an assortment of cards, photographs, several old keys, and scraps of paper. Odds and ends with no special place but too important to trash.

Marne went through the papers and found the number, written on a memo page that read HARRY LEWISON, CHIEF PHARMACIST, SANTA MONICA HOSPITAL.

With the paper in her hand, she went to the telephone and stood looking out over the Pacific, that calm body of water that could so quickly turn into a churning, threatening mass. And she felt her pulse speeding up, like yesterday when she was sprinting toward the sunrise. She had beaten her usual time by thirty-nine seconds. It was a good omen. As she punched in the numbers, Marne held her breath, wishing she knew a mantra or some other magical means to get her to paradise.

chapter TWO

"May I speak to Mrs. Kessler?"

"Hold the line. I'll see if I can find her." It was a man's voice, slightly quavering, and Marne heard in the background the commotion of things banging, children's giggles, a shriek, scraping sounds. Then one voice dominated, calling loudly, "No, no, Yossi, put that down. You can't have it. Here, take this pan—make us a pretend cake."

The same voice, harried and slightly hoarse, sounded in Marne's ear. "Yes? Who is this?"

"It's Marne, Aunt Carole."

The pause felt like a drumbeat. Marne held tight to the receiver, waiting. "Marne Lewison," she said.

"Marne. Is—is everything all right? Is everything fine?"

"Yes. We're fine." Now that the preliminaries were done, Marne felt blocked, as if she had hit a wall. How could she possibly put it? She wished she had written down notes the way her mom did before making a business call. "We're all fine," she said. "My mom has this great opportunity to go to Paris this summer, to show her designs and work with some other people. She's really excited about it."

"Well, that's terrific. I know your mom is very talented."

"Yes, and so we were talking about . . ."

"What will you be doing this summer?" her aunt asked.

"Well, that's the thing. I don't know. I thought maybe . . ."

"Why don't you come and visit us in Hawaii? The kids would love it. Especially Becca. She's my oldest, and she's got all these boys and babies to put up with."

It was like realizing the race is over and you've won, while your mind is still chanting, *"Reach, run, relax."*

"You're inviting me, Aunt Carole? Really?"

"Yes, really. Of course." Aunt Carole gave a slight laugh. "And, Marne, bring your guitar."

"My guitar?"

"We'd love to hear you play. We all love to sing."

"How do you know I play guitar?"

There was a pause, and the background noise, too, had stopped. "Well, when we were there I heard you playing in your room. We talked about it. Remember?"

"I—yeah. Sure." There was this blank moment, a space in memory. "I remember you cooked for us."

Her aunt laughed. "Yes, that sounds like me. I think I was pregnant with the twins. Even then, in my belly, they liked the music. I remember how they kicked."

Marne said, "I'll bring my guitar, Aunt Carole."

"Good. But you should know, I'm not called Carole anymore. My name is Chaya."

"Chaya," Marne repeated. "When did you change it?"

"About a year after I got married. I just didn't mention it to your mom. Didn't want to upset anyone."

"I never heard a name like that before," Marne said.

"It means 'life.' You know—like the toast. *L'chaim.* To life."

Marne became aware of her mother standing behind her, close. Her mom's eyes were bright, her hands reaching for the telephone as she mouthed the words, "Let me talk."

"Here's Mom. She wants to talk to you, Chaya."

Marne stood at the window, hearing the sounds of the neighborhood, the slamming of car doors, stray cats yowling, joggers and dog walkers and late-night shoppers out for a cup of coffee or a quart of milk. It was a small hub, Hermosa Beach, with its tightly nested houses, all competing for a sliver of view, a bit of ocean breeze. Her mother's conversation sounded stilted, with long pauses and little inflection.

"Of course, we would certainly appreciate it."

Marne turned to look at her mother. Her face was nearly expressionless, like a figure made from wax. In the shadowy light, she looked tired and drawn but still beautiful, with her auburn hair and slim, perfect nose. She wore pale tan slacks and a matching shirt; her clothes always matched.

"We manage. Thanks. No. We don't. How is your family? Good. I will. I won't. I'll let you know her flight. Oh? You have email? All right. Thanks, Carole."

"She changed her name," Marne said. "It's Chaya now."

Dad put away the paper and drew down the blinds. "What kind of a name is that?" he asked.

"It means 'life,'" Marne said.

"Probably Hebrew," Mom said. "Well, to each his own. Why would anyone want to change their name?"

"You did," Marne pointed out.

"That's different. I did it for professional reasons. Besides, have you ever heard of anyone named Nancie Jo who wasn't a bimbo? I don't know what my mother was thinking."

"She sounds very nice," Marne said. "She told me to bring my guitar."

"Well, then," her mother said briskly, "you should bring it, by all means."

She hated it when they ganged up on her, sat her down, and started in to "educate Marne," as if she was entirely clueless. What made it worse was their attempt to sound so unemotional, using shrink vocabulary. "If anyone tries to pressure you . . . You might want to use this as a learning experience . . . There's nothing wrong with letting people have their own beliefs. However, nobody has the right to inflict . . ."

"I get it, Mom," she finally said. "Look, I know Aunt Carole is a religious fanatic, so what? So, they pray a lot. She wears a weird thing on her head. All I want to do is go to Hawaii and run on the beach in the morning, maybe swim in the ocean and learn to surf."

"You do that, honey," said her father. "Nobody's trying

to influence you. It's wonderful of your aunt to take you in. It's just that some people . . ."

"Some people think when they've found something, you know, spiritual . . ."

"That they have a right to inflict it on others," finished her father.

Marne sat quietly, her hands in her lap, looking out into the foggy night. In the weeks since she had spoken to Carole, the matter had been shelved almost completely. *We are,* Marne thought, *so good at shelving things, at pretending to forget.* The truth was, she had told herself all the same concerns that her parents now offered. And yet, going to Hawaii was the only possible answer. She had wanted to stay home, but both her parents were adamant: she would never be left home alone at night, and Dad had to take some night shifts. Even in the daytime, they insisted, it's not good to be alone, ever. Not until you're grown. It seemed that they couldn't wait for her to grow up and leave them to their own lives.

They continued to explain about Carole—Chaya—about ritual and institutions, and Marne gritted her teeth and forced herself to remain silent. If she said nothing, they'd stop and she could get on with her packing. Nobody was going to inflict anything on her. Didn't they realize she had a mind of her own? Didn't they realize she wasn't the kind of person who'd crack under pressure?

Finally they let her go to finish her packing. But she still heard them through the walls.

"Maybe this wasn't such a good idea."

"Well, she has to learn to stand her ground. She's a practical kid."

"Mature for her age."

"Well, a big piece of her childhood was stolen from her."

"Nance. Don't. Please."

Now there was silence, and Marne wondered which was worse, the words or the silences. She put on her headphones and let the music of Tris and the Triplets soothe her. They were heavy on guitar, with Tris as the lead singer and composer. He gave her the kind of music that had answers, not for problems, but for feelings.

> Oh, oh, oh, how do I know the sound of the sea
> Is the best thing that could happen to me,
> Except being free to love you, love you, love you!

Only nine more hours, Marne thought as she packed her new bikini and matching wraparound, along with

leather sandals, shorts, running clothes, and several flowered skirts. She put her iPod carefully into her carry-on.
On her bookshelf were two paperbacks she hadn't read
yet, one mystery and a classic from the summer reading
list. She stuffed them into a corner of her bag and zipped
it shut.

She sat down on her bed, staring into space. A feeling
pulsed through her, a quickening, almost panic. *No. Resist. Don't take it. It's stupid and childish. It's a ridiculous
habit, an addiction.*

But habit prevailed. Habit soothed her like a warm
shower, like an embrace.

Bending down, Marne reached in between her mattress and box spring and brought out the slim book. She
held it in her hands for a long moment, feeling the smooth,
cool cover on her hot palms. Then she wrapped it in a
white T-shirt and placed it carefully on the bottom of her
suitcase. If Mom saw the book, she'd get that look on her
face. In the morning, first thing, she'd make a phone call
to the shrink.

With the book in place, Marne closed her suitcase,
ready for tomorrow, and freedom.

chapter THREE

Marne had only flown twice before, both times to Miami to visit Grandpa Irv and Grandmother Florence, who preferred to be called Nona. Nona wore her hair in an elfin cut, flat against her face, bleached ash-blond. Her lips, fingernails, and toenails were always perfectly painted in brilliant crimson or sparkling purple. Nona did not fly. She was deathly afraid of planes.

Strange, the memories that assaulted Marne as the plane soared through mounds and puffs of thick white clouds, emerging into the infinity of blue space. She loved to fly, to fantasize about the shapes in the sky and the world below, where thousands—no, millions—of people moved about their lives, each altered and urged by events they could hardly fathom, and yet they continued. She wished she knew the words for this idea. If she were to write a song, would it be about courage?

The flight attendant came by with her regulation smile and a tray of drinks. Marne took a Coke and a bag of pretzels. She savored the flavors. Not often was she out on her own like this. Even the woman beside her, who slept with her mouth open, emitting small grunts now and then, didn't faze her, nor did the lanky man sitting at the window, wearing oily-smelling overalls and heavy work shoes. She was dressed in her new jeans and a pink shirt, pink being her favorite color, defiance to the fashion "experts" who advised redheads to wear mostly earth colors. Marne loved peach and pink, with a touch of green. *Might that,* she wondered, *become a song?*

Her notebook lay in her bag, filled with scribbles, snatches of songs. She reached for the small pad and a stubby pencil and wrote: "Peach, pink, and green, where have I seen this combination? I can almost taste it, fruits and peppermint leaves. . . ."

Nothing else came to her mind. It was always like this: a beginning, a feeling surging over her, the hope that this time it would all merge into a complete and beautiful song. How did songwriters do it? How did they make it all come together? She had tried, dozens of times, hundreds of times. The scraps filled her wastebasket, and phrases crowded the margins of her notebooks. Something was always missing, but even in the night, while she slept, words washed through Marne's mind, phrases forming and reshaping themselves, so that sometimes when she awakened in the morning, she actually thought she had done it. But when she went to write down the song, it had vanished.

She put on her headset, turned to jazz, and leaned back as far as the seat would permit. Soon, behind her closed eyes, visions paraded—Grandpa Irv, Nona, the Florida coast with its cabanas and countless restaurants, the telephone call. "I'd come, Nancie Jo, darling, but you know I don't fly. . . ." All the telephone calls came in on the speaker so that everyone could hear, just in case there was a ransom call.

Her mother's face was white and sunken. "Of course, of course," she said. "Mother, I've got to go. We need to keep the phone clear."

The cops set up recording devices in Marne's dining room, claiming every space. She had walked in to find everything in chaos and forever changed.

Marne had been away at camp. The director called Marne into her office. "My dear child," she began, and Marne had wondered at the strangeness of those words, for the director, a freckled, reed-thin woman, had always until now addressed them as "campers" or by their cabin names, "Seneca" or "Dakota" or "Cherokee." They were big on Indian lore and on crafts. Stupid crafts, collages made with beads and colored sand and beans, like she'd done in kindergarten, but now she was ten.

"My dear child, I hate to be the one to tell you this, but your parents have sent for you. You are to leave immediately. They are sending a car."

"A car?"

Marne had written a letter home, telling them how bored she was at camp. Most of the girls giggled and gossiped or cried. She had expected races and competitions, real hikes, not those three-quarter-mile strolls around the putrid lake.

Naturally she thought they had sent for her to bring her home. Maybe they'd found a real camp, where kids could ride horses and play tennis and do some rock climbing.

"Go and pack up, my dear. Your counselor will help you."

So she had rushed to pack her things, carried them in Dad's big duffel bag to the front of the lodge, where soon the car rolled up. It was a station wagon, driven by Mr. Fortas, a neighbor. He had a strange look on his face, an arrested smile, a deep flush.

"Hey, Marne," he said, "did they tell you what it's about?"

"They just said I'm going home. Why didn't my dad come?"

"He's—busy, Marne. He's working with some people." Mr. Fortas drove too fast down the twisting mountain road, and Marne strained against the seat belt to keep her balance.

"But why am I going home?"

"They want you with them. Look, your mom will explain. How was camp?"

Much later that night, after the cops left and the neighbors dispersed, and the emptiness was all that remained, Marne had lain in her bed as still as a stone, unable to cry. At last she got up, turned on the light, and went to her bookshelf above the built-in desk. She knew exactly what she wanted and what she needed. She had read the book many times before, always puzzled by its meaning. Now she knew.

She found the book immediately and pulled it from the shelf. She sat down with it on the carpet, her legs outstretched in a wide V. The title seemed to blink at her: *Outside Over There*. The pictures had always held her entranced: pictures of goblins, of a little girl waiting, looking out to sea. And the goblins came and took the baby away. Marne had stuffed the book in between her mattress and box spring. She never wanted to look at it again. And yet she did—again and again and again.

Now, as she sat in the plane with the clouds moving around her in a slow, hypnotic dance, the words came back to her, haunting as ever: "So the goblins came. They pushed their way in and pulled baby out. . . ." She had memorized the words long ago, memorized every picture in the book, as if to find some clue to what really happened to Jody, her little sister, while she was away at camp.

The meal, set out on their trays, made her neighbors suddenly talkative. The man sat up and said, "Hey, this doesn't look half bad. It looks totally bad!" He laughed heartily at his joke. Marne only smiled. She wasn't good at small talk.

The woman turned to her and said brightly, "You going for vacation? All by yourself? Maybe for a job? You look so young. But looks are deceiving."

"I'm going to visit my aunt for the summer. She lives on Oahu."

"Well, isn't that glorious? I say, there's nothing like family. I've just been to Wisconsin to visit mine. We have these glorious reunions. Oh, we used to fight like hounds, but blood is thicker than water." She was homely, her hair damaged and frizzy, her eyes pale blue, devoid of lashes.

"Yes," Marne said faintly.

The woman rattled on, secure in her audience. "There were five of us. Brother passed away last year. Cancer. Three weeks after he was diagnosed, he was gone. Well, I always say, the good Lord knows when your time is up, and there's nothing we can do about it. I'm not scared of flying, are you?"

"No, not at all," said Marne.

"I thought you knew the Lord!" the woman exclaimed, beaming.

Marne clamped on her headset. The woman pulled a lapful of pale green yarn from her satchel and began with swift movements on her handiwork, a large blanket. The pattern looked like a spider's web. Marne watched the woman's hands, watched the yarn being formed into shapes. It looked difficult.

The woman smiled and took up her repartee. "So, how long will you be in the islands?"

"All summer."

"Oh, you'll love the islands," the woman said. "I came

eighteen years ago, just for vacation. Met my husband and we got married that fall. He's part Hawaiian, part Samoan. Our kids," she said, laughing, "are Heinz 57 varieties. Me, I'm part Irish, Scotch, French, and about one-sixteenth Apache and one-sixteenth Jew. Looks to me like you're Irish, your eyes, you know, and the red hair. Are you Irish?"

"I don't think so," said Marne. Some Russian, German, maybe Polish, too. *One hundred percent Jew,* she wanted to say, but it seemed irrelevant, like all this small talk had been. The flight attendant announced the beginning of the movie, and Marne gratefully turned to watch the screen.

People and images rushed past her. Brown-skinned little children, women in flowing skirts, men in flowered shirts and flip-flops. A woman with long black hair and a poster-like smile stood in their path. Flower leis cascaded from her arms. "Welcome! Aloha!" She rushed forward to embrace the tour people, who smiled affably at the surprise.

Marne saw the woman from the plane being greeted by an enormous man who waddled up to her with an orchid lei and gave her an exuberant hug. Marne marveled that ordinary, ugly people could stay in love for eighteen years.

Marne found her luggage, lifted it onto a luggage cart, and went outside, where the air was warm and fragrant and people hurried into cars and buses. She stood waiting for ten minutes, fifteen. What if Aunt Carole never came? Where would she go? Can a person just walk out of their life and *leave*? The idea was startling and strangely appealing. To begin fresh, to be entirely on her own, never to have to explain anything or try to patch anything together.

She waited and waited outside the terminal, watching people, checking her wristwatch with growing irritation. She was thirsty and hot. She felt like an immigrant, standing there with her bags, reluctant even to go inside for a soda for fear of missing her aunt.

"Someone coming for you?"

Marne whirled around. It was a young man in an army uniform. He looked strong but boyish with his close-cropped hair and eager smile. "I just saw you here ever since we landed, and I thought maybe . . ."

"My aunt's coming for me," Marne said, her heart thumping. She did not speak readily to strangers, especially boys. "She's just a little late, I guess."

"It's awfully hot just standing here," he said. "Can I get you a soda?"

"Oh, no," Marne said quickly. "I'm fine."

"My brother's picking me up," he said. "But he lives on the other end of the island. And he never did learn to tell time."

"I hope he learned to drive," Marne said lightly. The warm trade winds and the scent of flowers made everything seem slightly unreal.

"He improvises. Hey, my name is Chet Harrington," he said, thrusting out his hand. "I'm from Ohio, stationed here in Honolulu now."

"Tough duty, huh," Marne said. She felt light and happy, not at all strange. Chet seemed to be about eighteen, not that much older than she. He'd been annoyed, too, at being stranded. It was easy talking to him, and she felt content: *I can do this!* The way Chet smiled at her made her glad she had worn the pink shirt and her favorite silver hair clip, to keep the hair up and back from her face.

Marne took his hand, smiling. "I'm Marne Lewison, from L.A."

"L.A.! So I guess you hang around with movie stars."

"Oh, sure. Yesterday I had breakfast with J. Lo and

lunch with Madonna. Hectic social schedule. I came here for a rest."

"So, you play the guitar," he said, patting the guitar case.

"I try," Marne said modestly.

"You know that group Tris and the Triplets? They have this great song. . . ."

"I love them!" Marne exclaimed. "I listen to them all the time."

He said, "Look, I'm going to get myself a soda. Can I bring one back for you?"

"Sure. Actually, I'm—"

"Marne! Marne! Hey—come on. Get in. I can't park here." It was a dark van, with all the windows open and a woman leaning across the girl in the front seat. The woman's hair was copper-colored, shoulder length, and she tossed it aside with a vigorous motion as she called again. "Marne! Is that you?"

Marne rushed to the van. "Aunt Chaya?"

"I'm sorry I'm late. I had to do an errand. Let's put your luggage in the rear."

Before Marne knew it, Chet had brought her bags over to the van and stood close beside her, grinning. "I guess we'll have to take a rain check on that soda."

"Yes, but thanks anyhow."

Chaya jumped out from the van. She motioned the girl into the backseat, wiped the baby's mouth, gave instructions for loading up the van. Her movements were vigorous and quick, her features firm. "Thank you, thank you," she said as Chet hoisted up Marne's bags and the guitar. "We have to go. I've still got errands to do. Sorry I was so late." She reached into the van and pulled out three flower leis, two lavender, one white. She slipped the leis over Marne's head, saying, "Welcome, Marne. Aloha," gave a quick peck to her cheek and said, "Come on. Let's go."

Marne glanced at Chet, his expression a mixture of amusement and regret. "So, have a good vacation," he said.

Impulsively, Marne took one of the leis from around her neck and slipped it over Chet's head. "Aloha," she said, smiling.

"No kiss?" Chet murmured.

"Come on, Marne!" Chaya called loudly. "Get in! Buckle up!"

"Wiki wiki," yelled the little boy as Marne got into the van, her face burning from the heat of the car and from annoyance. She felt like a child, being dragged away. Chaya gunned the motor and sped out onto the boulevard.

She's mad I gave one of her leis away, Marne thought. Too bad. Mom wouldn't be mad; she'd think it was nice.

"You came on a plane, *wiki wiki,*" shouted the little boy in back.

"Stop screaming, Yossi!" Chaya called. "Talk nicely to your cousin, talk like a person."

"What's *wiki wiki*?" Marne asked.

"It means 'fast' in Hawaiian," said the girl solemnly.

"That's Becca," Chaya explained, intent on driving, taking the curves with a certain fury. "The little screamer is Yossi. Back there with him is Nissim. He's seven, Yossi is nearly three, and the baby, Bennie, is nineteen months. Kids, say hi to your cousin Marne."

Marne glanced into the backseat, where the two little boys and the baby sat with their large brown eyes fastened upon her. Only Becca said a faint hi, then giggled self-consciously. Yossi's hair fell nearly to his shoulders. The golden curls would make anyone think he was a girl, except for the *kippa* on his head and the overalls. He stared out the window, counting red cars, an intense competition that he was waging with seven-year-old Nissim.

"Four-leven-teen!" Yossi screamed, and Nissim answered, "You don't know how to count, Yossi," to which the younger boy yelled, "I do, too, one, two, three, four, five, six, seven, eight, nine, eleven!"

"Okay," Nissim sighed. He gave Marne a long, martyred look. "He always forgets the *ten*."

"He'll learn," Marne murmured. Nissim's face was so serious, his hair most like her own, a reddish brown.

Yossi, Nissim. Strange names. How would she ever remember them?

Marne took a deep breath, thinking of the woman on the plane and her easy chatter. "How many children do you have, Aunt Chaya?" she asked, feigning real interest.

"Seven, thank God," Chaya said briskly. "The twins, Esti and Elias, are home with Yitz. And my oldest boy, Jonathan, is still in New York with his grandparents. He'll be here next week."

The names rolled through Marne's mind. "Yitz is your husband?" Not Itch, she thought.

"Yes. It's actually Isaac—Yitzhak, in Hebrew. Yitz for short."

"But he's not short," said Becca with a slight chuckle. "He's very tall."

"How old are you, Becca?" Marne asked, turning to look at her cousin, searching for some family resemblance.

But there was none. Becca had smooth, copper-colored hair, a wide brow, and large brown eyes. Her skin, smooth and satiny, bore no hint of freckles. Marne noticed her long jean skirt and limp white blouse. More colorful clothes, she thought, would do her good.

"Twelve," Becca said. "I was born the same year as your—"

Chaya interrupted. "Becca, reach into that cooler and give Marne an orange soda. She must be dehydrated by now."

Marne's heart hammered. If Jody were here, the two of them would already be giggling and whispering secrets. Jody was like that, with her big smile and those red frizzy curls. Women in the supermarket called her "sweetie," even when they didn't know her, and they reached out to pat her hair.

Marne felt a hand on her shoulder. "Here's your soda, Marne," Becca said softly. "You can sleep with me in my room. Do you want to, Marne?"

"Okay, Becca," Marne said. She reached into her bag for her iPod. Maybe Chaya would think it was rude, but she might as well let them know she was not going to be dragged into their lives.

Marne listened to Tris and the Triplets while she

gazed out the window at the palm trees, the modern buildings with glistening windows, and the distant ocean, a slate-blue color. As soon as she got to the house, she'd put on her bathing suit and go to the beach, even if she had to catch a bus. She needed to get away.

But Chaya stopped at a supermarket, then at a produce stall and a print shop. Marne fetched things, loaded up the van, held the baby, wiped his dirty face again and again, thinking only of the beach, free time, a good run.

"Now, home," Chaya finally said. It was nearly dark.

Home was a small cottage, the sandy yard dotted with scrubby bushes and scattered toys. Chaya pushed the door open. Immediately Marne felt the assault like a vibration. The phone and fax rang simultaneously. A disheveled-looking woman ran up to Chaya with a list in her hand. The baby howled. Chaya picked him up, held him on her hip. Yossi, the almost-three-year-old, dumped a box of puzzle pieces out on the floor, and Yitz appeared in the doorway. "Welcome to our home, Marne!" he said exuberantly. "We're so glad to have you!" He was a tall man with broad shoulders and a shy smile, his pink lips contrasting with the dark beard.

"Thanks," Marne said, trying not to stare at the long fringes that hung down from his waist or the rumpled dress shirt. His baggy black slacks and black skullcap made him look like a deacon from the Middle Ages. Rimless glasses were perched on his nose.

"How are your parents? Did you have a good flight?" Yitz smiled, and Marne could see where the children got their twinkling eyes. "The children were so excited to hear you'll be staying. Aloha!"

She felt dumbstruck, having expected—what? A Bible-toting rabbi? Someone who chanted when he talked and used long, sonorous phrases? Yitz sounded like a New Yorker, his vowels long and rounded. He swung his arms when he spoke, filling the room with his presence and his ready smile.

He snatched up Baby Bennie, yanked up his trousers, and held him over his shoulder, giving Chaya the day's news while she unloaded groceries, chucked things into bins and baskets, tossed burgers into a large skillet.

"Frances called. Her parents are visiting. I invited them for *Shabbos* dinner. Five more. And Aaron is bringing two friends from the mainland. Carl wants to know whether we want to help plan a Hawaiian holiday party for December, along with the other groups on the island. I told him we'd discuss it. I have another *bas mitzvah* girl.

She's coming next week with her older sister. Kahn is the name—maybe you know them. The sister might want to study with you. I left the number. We got two more calls for day camp. I left the numbers. The garage door seems to be stuck again. Do you have the warranty?"

To everything Chaya gave an answer, with a vigorous, decisive nod. The twins yelled and trudged back and forth, trying to help. Yossi manipulated a small, child-size broom with vigor, yelling, "Clean up! Clean up, kids!" Things rattled and fell, something broke. A white-haired man appeared at the door with a box of papayas. "Thank you, Sol! You're a lifesaver!" Chaya exclaimed, showing him into the kitchen. "Marne," she called, "this is our friend Sol. He's a marvel—hikes two miles every day and brings us fresh fruit from his place. I don't think we could manage without him. Sit down, sit down, have some iced tea and a piece of cake. Becca! Bring Sol a nice slice of cake."

The man sat down, beaming all around, like a grand-father on loan. He nodded to Marne and smiled. "Hello! You must be new. Welcome!" He regarded Marne for a long moment. "My wife had hair like yours," he said. "Auburn, she called it. I called it red." He laughed and stretched out his hand as if to touch Marne's hair, then he drew back.

"Thanks." It seemed to be all she was saying, *thanks*. She thought of her grandmother Nona and grandfather Irv, the immaculate house on the golf course, how they met friends at the clubhouse for lunch or cocktails and nobody ever dropped in. Her own house was as silent as a cave, except when Marne was watching TV or listening to music or playing guitar. Did her father mind the sudden quiet, she wondered, or was he glad?

Outside in the small yard, Marne tried to call him on her cell phone. She rang the hospital, the house, his cell. No answer. At last she left a message, making her voice cheerful. Good old Marne, nothing bothers her. She's an adaptable kid.

"Hi, Daddy! I just wanted you to know I got here just fine. It was a good flight. Aunt Chaya and the kids are . . ." She hesitated. "Just fine. Call me when you can!"

In the large kitchen/family room, Sol was finishing his cake. Then he began to sing a wordless tune, slapping at the tabletop. Little Yossi did a sudden dance, kicking, sliding, whirling. *"Ya-ya-ya, de-da-da-da-da-dah!"*

"Marne plays the guitar!" Chaya offered, passing

through. "Maybe you'll play for us later. The kids love music."

"I'd love to," Marne said, her mind racing over the pop songs she knew, none of them exactly right. What she needed for this crowd was an accordion or a harmonica and an Austrian polka, like her dad's uncle used to play. Marne vaguely remembered him, a large, obese man with a sagging double chin, and how his chin wobbled when he sang.

Baby Bennie tried to keep up. The faster he went, the lower his pants slid, until they fell down around his ankles and he sat on the floor, howling out his frustration. Becca scooped him up. She tugged the pants back onto his bottom and, with a quick kiss, launched him again.

Five-year-old Esti flapped around in a red outfit with purple plastic shoes and a tattered purple boa around her neck. She struck a pose and started to sing. Yossi and Elias chased each other around the room. The threads hanging from their waists swung wildly as they ran. *This is a madhouse,* Marne thought, dismayed. She was glad when Chaya pointed to the cabinet and said, "Marne, would you help Becca set the table?" She needed some purpose, some respite.

Chaya scooped up Bennie, who was howling again. She wiped his hands with a cloth, leaning toward her guest. "Sol, won't you stay for dinner? Niss, go get some soda from the garage. Then wash up, everyone. Wash up for bread!"

Marne watched as they lined up to wash at a small sink at the side of the room, obviously a bar. The glass shelves above the sink held a single bottle of wine and a stack of plastic cups. "Want to wash?" Esti said, hopping on one foot.

"I already did," Marne answered.

Yitz seated her at the middle of the table, opposite Sol. "We're so happy to have you here!" he said, beaming.

Dinner passed in a haze of commotion. Platters and bowls were heaped with meat, vegetables, pasta. "May I have a glass of milk?" Marne asked innocently.

For an instant everything ceased. "Ha!" Sol exclaimed, leaning back in his chair.

Esti piped up, "We don't—"

"We have juice," Chaya said briskly, "or caffeine-free Coke."

"Coke, please," Marne replied. Questions resonated in her mind, unspoken. It was all too confusing, too sudden, and she felt very, very far from home.

At last Marne dropped into the bed beside Becca's. The sheets were cool, the bed narrow. "Want to tell stories?" Becca asked in a small voice.

"No," Marne sighed, wishing only for sleep and sweet oblivion.

From outside, she heard the wind slapping the palm leaves with a constant *swish, swish*. The scent of ginger blossoms seeped into her semi-dreams. Mingled with the fragrance came soft voices, murmuring in rhythm, like a song, rising and falling, a peaceful cadence that could only be the voice of prayer. Deep in her consciousness Marne was aware of Becca and Chaya, whispering from the bed beside hers: *"Shema Yisrael . . ."* The words were familiar, though she had not heard them for a long, long time.

chapter FOUR

Marne ran through the rain forest of Kauai toward the waterfall, its rushing waters cascading down between giant ferns and orchid plants. *Reach. Soar. Breathe.* She checked her watch. Her time was improved by nearly two minutes—*reach, soar!* The splashing became a torrent. A helicopter roared over her. She felt smothered, hot.

Groaning, Marne pushed at the thing that had landed on her chest. Esti and Eli were waging an assault on her bedclothes. Esti's small body lay on top of her.

"Hey! What are you doing?"

Esti giggled. Her mouth was rimmed with red juice, and her tongue and little teeth glistened. "Hi! Wake up, sleepyhead!"

"You're heavy," Marne said, sitting up.

"Esti! Elias!" came Chaya's voice from the other room. "Leave Marne alone! Maybe she wants some privacy."

Marne laughed. Privacy? Eli was poking through her

suitcase, holding her iPod, asking, "Can I hear this? Is it Uncle Moshe?"

"No, it's—something else," Marne said, glancing to the side where Becca stood in front of an old-fashioned pitcher and basin, pouring water on her fingertips.

Marne sat up, surveying the room, the basin. "What's that?" she asked. The twins giggled. *"Negel vasser!"* they screamed, pushing at each other.

"Leave Marne alone!" scolded Becca as Esti and Eli pounced on the bed again. "That's no way to treat a guest. Go on."

To Marne's surprise, they darted out, and Becca gave her a smile. "Good morning."

"What's *negel vasser*?" Marne asked. She felt like an imposter in this room, with its miniature dressing table and clothing and books and shoes strewn all around.

Becca crinkled her nose. "I'm not sure. It's just something we do to wash away the night."

Marne threw back the covers. "Wash away the night? You mean, like evil spirits? Ghosts?" She felt stricken, alarmed. Her mother had shouted it, finally, in disgust, "They reek of superstition."

Becca bit her lip. "I can't explain it. You'd better ask my dad."

Marne stared at Becca, at her helplessness. She sighed. "Okay. What time is it?"

"Seven."

"That's ten in California!" Marne exclaimed, and she jumped out of bed. At home, she was always the first one up, running along the shore, then home to the silent house to start the coffee while her parents still slept.

Marne made her way to the bathroom, maneuvering between toy ducks and boats, clumps of discarded underwear, a painted step stool, and wet towels. A pail in the corner was mercifully covered. Marne didn't have to wonder what it contained. She marveled at the disarray, not that she was the neatest person in the world—but still. The soap bar slid from her hand, a mass of jelly. *Kids!* At home, she had her own bathroom. She hoped, for Chaya's sake, that there was another bathroom in the house.

Back in the bedroom, Marne took a quick inventory. Becca's clothes hung on knobs, posts, and hooks. She was also something of a scavenger, evident from the piles of junk she must have gathered from the beach—metal screws and bolts, seashells, bits of driftwood, and large brown pods.

"So, what are you doing this morning?" Marne asked.

"Mom runs a summer day camp at the beach," Becca

said. "We have a little bungalow and stuff. I'm the head junior counselor."

Marne stared. "Who takes care of the other kids?"

"Oh, we bring them along."

Marne picked up the ginger lei with its defeated, browning blossoms and tossed it into the wastebasket. She stacked her few books and iPod neatly on the nightstand. Quickly, Marne unpacked her clothes and filled the two empty drawers. She stood her guitar up in a corner, then got dressed in her shorts, a tank top, and running shoes.

"Where are you going?" Becca asked, pulling on her skirt. Faded pink with a large ruffle that came down to her ankles, it looked like something from the Goodwill store. If Kim were here, she'd wrinkle her nose and roll her eyes. Whenever they saw weird-looking people at the mall, Kim would whisper, "Obviously from Mars."

"I'm going running," Marne replied, starting her stretches.

"How far do you go?"

"About five miles."

"Wow!"

"See ya!" Marne waved and ran through the kitchen,

with its chaos of children delving into cupboards, pulling out boxes of cereal. Esti was cutting a peach into tiny cubes. Elias was hoisting potatoes from a bag to his mother's outstretched hands. Baby Bennie sat in his high chair, singing and banging out a tune on his tray, where the scattered Cheerios bounced and jiggled.

"Morning!" called Chaya. "Did you sleep well?"

"Great," replied Marne. "I'm going for a run."

Yossi, his face and his long curls streaked with something Marne did not care to identify, attached himself to her right leg. "I wanna go!" he shrieked. "Take me with you!"

"Yossi, let go of her," commanded Chaya, turning from the cupboard.

"Later," Marne said, disengaging herself. Yossi's lip quivered. She gave him a quick pat, surprised at the silkiness of his hair.

"Later I'll read you a story!" Marne promised. She ran out, filled with a sense of purpose. She had pondered this beginning just before she fell asleep. Should she let herself go like a piece of driftwood, hang around, and fit into Chaya's schedule? She wasn't looking forward to a repetition of yesterday, with miles of driving, packing up the car, hauling groceries, mopping up spills. She intended to help, of course. She would be pleasant. But she had a life, after all.

Mom's words had clattered through her dreams: *"They live a different lifestyle."* Marne hadn't realized exactly what that meant. Now she was beginning to understand. She thought of the nursery rhyme, *"There was an old woman who lived in a shoe. She had so many children, she didn't know what to do."* That was Chaya, all right. Except that she wasn't old. And she did seem to know what she was doing.

Outside in the sandy yard, Marne stretched, inhaled deeply, invigorated by the broad expanse of sky, the wide beach, and the thought of freedom, beautiful freedom. Nobody to offer clipped remarks, no almost fights followed by silence that fell as heavy as fog. She trotted along the narrow, sandy lane bordered with small houses, past a billowing mound of wild grass, and there it was, calm water and vast shore. True paradise.

A few runners were still coming in from their morning jog. Tomorrow, Marne vowed, she would be up in time to catch the sunrise, probably five a.m., six at the latest. She started slowly, feeling the gradual sense of power, reaching that point of transcendence where worries evaporated and only pure energy remained. She imagined herself a cat, a lion, stretching her limbs without effort, a horse galloping near the shore, an Olympic contender going for the gold.

At the edge of her vision she saw several boys with their boards, gauging the surf. Their bodies were bronze, wet, and gleaming. *Beautiful!* If Kim had been here, she would have grabbed Marne's hand and made her slow down, showing off, getting the boys to notice. It was easy for Kim to talk to boys.

Looking back on her meeting Chet at the airport, Marne felt triumphant. Kim would cheer her on. But she'd ask, "Did you find out where he was staying? Are you going to see him again? Did he take your phone number?" *No, no, no. Of course not.*

Marne ran barefoot, feeling the warm, soft sand between her toes. A constant breeze fanned her face and her body, soothed her muscles, so that the run seemed effortless. At home, often a sharp chill in the air and clammy fog made her tighten up. Here, her legs and arms felt loose, relaxed, moving with the flow of the warm wind and the sweet rustle of palms. People along the way invariably smiled or waved to her, as if she were a long-awaited guest and welcome here in paradise.

Marne walked the last quarter mile, savoring the sights and smells and sounds of Hawaii. She turned in at the lane, and then she stretched in the sandy yard, cooling off. The whole day lay ahead of her. She inhaled deeply, gauging the possibilities. She'd go swimming, maybe borrow a surfboard or take a lesson. She'd lie in the sun, listening to her music. Maybe she'd bring her guitar to the beach. She and Becca might take the bus to Waikiki, browse in the shops, look at the trinkets in the jewelry stalls, following the tourists. She and Kim loved going to the mall and trying on clothes. Once they spent hours trying on wigs. When the clerk got annoyed, Kim actually produced tears. "I'll soon be needing this," she had whispered, implying hair loss, cancer, the works. Later they admitted that it was outrageous, giggling wildly. "She's a kick!" Marne's mom always said. "A little goofy, but who isn't at that age?"

Marne hurried into the house, calling, "Hi, everybody!" But the house was quiet. A trail of toys and a few Cheerios remained, witnesses to the former chaos. Marne helped herself to a large banana muffin from a package. In the refrigerator she found a carton of orange juice and, after rummaging through several cabinets, a glass.

From the den Marne heard a low, rumbling voice, the

scattered words, ". . . the Ba'al Shem Tov emphasized serving God with joy. The first duty of man was to seek God . . . not too difficult, because God is everywhere in the universe. . . ."

Marne knocked softly. She waited, her body still damp from her run.

Yitz leaped up. "Hey! Good morning, Marne! Did you rest well?"

"Yes, thanks. Where is everyone?" Marne pushed open the door and stepped inside. The portable air conditioner emitted a cold blast. Marne shivered.

"They've all gone to day camp," Yitz said. He looked over at the window. "Usually Nissim goes, too, but he's here with me."

Now Marne noticed that the boy was curled into a large chair, his face down on the leather cushion. He glanced up, his eyes puffy, nose running.

"What's wrong, Niss?" Marne said.

"Nothing," he mumbled, wiping his nose with the back of his hand.

"You can tell Marne," Yitz said. "She's your cousin. Maybe she also has a pet."

"What is it?" Marne asked.

"My fish," said Nissim. "It's lying on the top of the water. Turned over. Dead."

"Your fish died? How come?"

Nissim mumbled, "Esti and Eli killed it."

"They overfed it," Yitz explained.

"Now Arnold will die, too," Nissim said.

Marne glanced from Nissim to Yitz. "Who's Arnold?"

"His other fish," Yitz said. "He thinks it will die of loneliness."

"It's possible," Marne said softly. She walked closer to Nissim. He gave her a sidelong glance.

"You're not *tznius*," he muttered, looking away.

"Never mind, Nissim," his father said sternly. "You don't say that to a guest."

"Say what?" Marne asked.

Yitz stood up and turned off the CD. "Nissi, I told you I'll take you later to buy another fish. I can't go now," he explained to Marne. "I'm expecting a mother and her boy who want *bar mitzvah* lessons."

"Why can't Marne take me?" the boy said, rubbing his eyes. "By the time you take me, Arnold will be dead!"

"Look, Marne isn't here to do chores," Yitz said. "This is her vacation."

Nissim turned his face down onto the cushion. His back and shoulders heaved.

"I wouldn't mind taking him," Marne murmured. "Where's the pet store?"

"At the mini-mall about a mile from here. Do you drive?"

"I've got my learner's permit."

"Then you need to have a licensed driver with you." Yitz pulled at his lower lip. "I don't suppose—no. Forget it. He can wait."

"I don't mind walking. Would he walk with me?"

Nissim shot up out of the chair, grabbing Marne's hand. "Will you really take me? Now? Will you get a wife for Arnold?"

"Sure," Marne said, wondering how much such a wife would cost. She had brought two hundred dollars to last all summer, plus a credit card for emergencies. She hadn't planned on buying a fish. But Yitz had already reached into his pocket, and from a money clip he peeled a ten-dollar bill. "That should cover it," he said. "Next door to the pet store is an ice cream shop. They have a few kosher treats. Nissi will show you."

Marne sighed. Everything was so complicated. Kosher

ice cream. Whoever heard of it? She turned. Directly opposite Yitz's desk was a framed picture of a man's face, half smiling. "Is that your father?" Marne asked.

Yitz looked surprised. "It's the Rebbe. The Lubavitcher Rebbe. We are his emissaries, Chaya and I."

"Just you two?"

Yitz smiled. "No, there are hundreds, thousands of us, all over the world. We set up Chabad houses to bring the Rebbe's teachings to people with schools and prayer services."

"You convert people?"

Yitz shook his head. "We bring Jews back to their Jewish roots. Back to *Yiddishkeit*. We show them the real Judaism, from the old days. Tradition."

Marne nodded. "There's a Chabad place near our house. I see the men walking sometimes, but they don't look at me."

"Well, they're being modest, *tznius*."

"This Rebbe," Marne said, glancing at the picture. "Where does he live?"

"He died a few years ago. He lived in Crown Heights, Brooklyn. There are many stories about the Rebbe, his saintliness."

"I thought Jews don't have saints."

"Quite right. We call them *tzaddikim*. Wise and holy men and women."

"Women, too?"

"Oh, certainly. Women are considered inherently more spiritual than men."

Nissim took her hand, pulling slightly. "Come on!" he urged.

"Okay. I'll be back in a minute," Marne said, and went to wash her hands and face and under her arms. She felt sticky and sweaty from her run and from the growing heat outside.

"Let's go," she said, taking Nissim's hand.

He pursed his lips, looking down at the floor.

"What's wrong?"

"Nothing."

"Something's wrong. I can tell by your face," Marne insisted.

"Your—legs," the boy mumbled. "Everybody can see your legs."

"So?"

He sighed heavily, spread out his hands in the way of an old man delivering a lecture. "It's not *tznius,*" he said soberly.

54

Marne stood looking down at the little boy, his sorrowful face. Obviously, he wanted her to be dressed like his sister and his mom; he would be embarrassed by her. A stab of annoyance provoked her—almost—into snapping at Nissim, telling him to mind his own business. But Yitz walked by and grabbed the little boy by the arm and gave him a shake.

"Niss, don't you ever tell people what to do," he ordered. "Do you hear me?"

"It's cool," Marne said with a heavy sigh. "I don't mind changing. Really."

She came back wearing a pair of white capri pants and a pink shirt, tied at the waist. "Is this better?" she said testily, hand on her hip. "Now nobody can see my legs or hardly any skin. Okay?" She thought of Becca and that awful skirt, Chaya's high-necked blouse and long sleeves. Didn't they feel suffocated? Hadn't they noticed that on a tropical island, people dressed to be comfortable and cool?

"Okay, let's go," Nissim said. "I get to pick out the fish."

"Of course."

Nissim walked in silence beside her. Marne thought about initiating a conversation, but she was deterred by his relentless frown. Whatever she said, it would seem frivolous, out of place beside this very solemn child. At last he asked, "Do you have any pets?"

"No."

"Brothers?"

She took a deep breath. "No." She wanted to tell him about Jody, to show that she wasn't an only child, because in his world that must seem so abnormal. But that would evoke the inevitable stream of memories.

She asked, "When's your brother Jonathan coming home?"

"Eleven days and four hours, if you figure the day starts at seven in the morning."

"That's logical," said Marne. "I guess you miss him."

He didn't answer but pointed across the street where a large plate-glass window advertised PETS AND PET FOOD, EXOTICS, FISH AQUARIA.

Nissim murmured, "*Aquaria*. That means more than one aquarium."

They waited for the signal to change.

"We wrestle," Nissim added.

Marne understood. Little kids always leave gaps. Jody used to come up with the most irrelevant information. Odd fragments of Jody's chatter remained so clear in Marne's memory. Like the time Jody burst in giggling, "This man!

He had this bag and blew into it. Like this!" And Jody squealed in imitation of a bagpipe.

"You're nuts, Jody," Marne had yelled. "And next time you come in my room, you'd better knock. Or else I'll get a lock."

Jody had jumped up and down. "Knock, knock, lock, lock!"

And Marne had yelled at her, "Shut up, Jody! Get out!"

Now she asked Nissim, "Do you like to wrestle?"

"Not really. Sometimes it makes me barf."

"Why don't you tell him to quit?"

"Next time he goes," Nissim said solemnly, "I'm going with him."

"Where?"

"To New York. To *yeshiva*."

"*Yeshiva?* You mean, to school?"

He nodded. "*Yeshiva*. To learn. I have to stay there until I'm old."

"Older," Marne corrected. "What about Becca? Is she going away to school?"

Nissim shrugged, that gesture like an old man's, hands out, fingers splayed. "She's scared to leave home."

He broke away now and dashed into the pet store.

It took forever to choose. The clerk scooped the fish

into a small plastic bag. Nissim changed his mind and picked another fish, gold with a black dot on its head. "Fancier," he said. "Arnold wants a pretty wife. Look at those long fins! Don't you think long fins are prettier?"

"Definitely," Marne said. "Like long hair on a girl. Like Becca."

"You think the fish looks like Becca?" he exclaimed, smiling for the first time.

Marne laughed. "You better not tell that to Becca. And leave me out of it!" She put her hand on his shoulder and felt the small bones, the slim body. She gave Nissim the ten-dollar bill.

He looked up at the clerk and demanded, "We get *kama'aina* discount."

"Right-o," said the clerk.

"What's *mama'aina*?" Marne murmured.

"*Kama,*" Nissim corrected, laughing, showing his two large front teeth. "It's for living here, not being just a tourist."

"Oh." At last the mission was accomplished. Nissim allowed Marne to hold his fish while they walked to the ice cream store. He stood at the counter pondering his selection, crinkling up his forehead, squinting at the list of flavors. Finally he selected a vanilla frozen yogurt cone, with multicolored sprinkles topped with chopped peanuts.

"Are you sure you're satisfied?" Marne asked. She had had other plans for this day. Maybe Waikiki, lying on the beach, taking a bus to Pearl Harbor.

"Yes. Unless . . ."

"Only kidding! I'll have one scoop of rum raisin," she told the clerk, "and one of marble fudge."

"Not kosher," muttered Nissim.

She bent toward him. "What? What's wrong now?"

"You have to choose from the frozen yogurts."

"I do not!" Marne felt herself flushing, first with annoyance, then with embarrassment. She was sounding like a six-year-old and there behind her was one of the surfers from this morning. She realized, with astonishment, that she had memorized his sun-streaked hair, the dark blue bathing suit, and the medal he wore around his neck on a leather cord.

"Take vanilla," insisted Nissim.

"It's fat-free," said the surfer.

Marne could sense his grin. She bit her lip, feeling her own erratic heartbeat. Was that a hint? She sucked in her stomach. "Okay," she told the clerk. "Vanilla." It was not her favorite flavor.

chapter FIVE

Hi, Kim.

Wanted to call you but my cell is down and I couldn't get it fixed yet. Just now got to use the computer to email you. Most of the time it's in use. I'll try to get my phone fixed this week. I can't go anywhere cuz there's no buses and, of course, no car. There's a little strip mall in walking distance, but nothing really exciting. I keep thinking about the mall and I know you guys are hanging out there. Say hi to Bridgette at the Coffee Clique! I have NOT had a decent coffee since I got here. Oh, I met the cutest soldier at the airport! He offered to buy me a soda. There's an army base here. Lots of cute guys. You'll love it. When are you coming??

I've been running nearly every morning and see some cute surfers. The beach is cool, very hot, but cool—ha-ha.

I've been helping my aunt at her day camp. A bunch of little kids, all of 'em screaming and giggling. I'm starting to learn their names. One little guy named Monte is really cute. He wants to hold my hand all the time. He's scared of sand crabs and spiders. I caught a daddy longlegs and

showed him it wouldn't bite. He told his mom that I'm a su-
superhero. Isn't that cute? They are funny. One of the little
girls asked me whether she can go to the moon from Disneyland. They love jewelry. We make stuff out of pods and beads
and feathers.

When you come, bring me some flip-flops, please. You
can get them at Kit and Kaboodle in the mall. I'll pay you
back. Mine broke. I'd like black or dark green with a thick
sole.

You won't believe this, but I've only been swimming once!
There's a cove not very far from the house where we can go.
That is, Chaya and me and the girls. They don't swim with
boys. Don't ask me why. They are very uptight about things
like that.

Are these people from Mars???

Chaya and Becca wear these weird clothes. My aunt's
nice, tho she hardly has any time to talk. Actually, that's
okay, cuz what would I talk to her about? She's into day care
and kids and cooking and shopping. Food is huge, with all
those kids and on Friday about a thousand people here for
dinner. Actually, eighteen. I counted. They have guests all
the time. I mean, like, more than anyone, even you and your
sisters. Friday they keep *Shabbos,* which is Jewish Sabbath
(in case you didn't know), and they don't cook or answer the
phone or even turn on the lights! Who knew? I went to wash
my hair Friday night before going to sleep, and it was, like,

a major uproar, which I didn't get, cuz water is in the pipes anyhow, isn't it? But they don't want the water heater to go on. It's considered work. I don't get it—how much work is it to turn on a faucet? I was really bummed. I actually cried, tho I didn't mean to. I was just so mad, and then I got so embarrassed. Becca kept trying to explain it and make me feel better, and I actually told her to shut up and leave me alone. I thought she'd run and tell her mom and that would be the end of my visit to "paradise." But she just went to sleep and the next day everything was normal. Except that my hair was still dirty. Like my mom said, they have a different lifestyle. Boy, do they ever.

Saturday we went to *shul*. That is a service where they sing and pray a lot. I mean a lot!!! Even the kids have to be quiet, but of course they aren't. Yossi—he's nearly three—he rides this little plastic bike up and down the lobby, making noises, driving everyone crazy. The *shul*—that is the synagogue, in case you didn't know (I didn't know!)—is held in an old broken-down hotel in a room just off the lobby. Across from it is a Coke machine. You can imagine people going to get a Coke and looking at us as if we were from—yeah—Mars.

But after the prayers (which last forever!) they all have lunch. People sing at the table. Really! It's like camp. Some of the people were really nice and asked me all about L.A. and my family, and then they said, "Where do you *daven*?" which

I finally figured out means, "Where do you go to synagogue in L.A.?" So I looked pretty stupid when I said I don't usually go, but they were nice about it and nobody hassled me. One lady told me how she never used to go, but then she met Chaya and Yitz and now she is "so connected." Everyone is either "connected" or "on the path." But most of them look pretty normal, except a few guys who wear those black suits and big hats. My uncle is one of those. But he's cool. The afternoon was okay. We walked on the beach and talked to people and there were dogs racing around, playing Frisbee. Then we went back and played about a hundred games of Chutes and Ladders and Hi Ho! Cherry-O, and I felt like a little kid. The oldest boy, Jonathan, isn't even home yet from school. He's coming next week. I played chess with the seven-year-old, and he beat me. I guess that tells you something about my mental age, ha-ha.

I wanted to play my guitar. They said they all love music, but Yitz looked uncomfortable and later Becca told me he doesn't listen to girls singing solo. Women don't sing alone in front of men. They think it's not modest. Does any of this make sense to you? After all, Chaya told me to bring my guitar.

I sleep with Becca. She finally cleaned her room on Friday, even put flowers on the desk. Becca thinks I'm Wonder Woman cuz I run five miles a day. I wish I could get her to run. She's getting chubby, like us when we were in sixth grade, until we decided to take control of our bodies. That is, you decided, and I should thank you for it. Thank you!

I really miss you. When are you coming? I'll try to get my cell fixed and call you this week. Don't even try to call me at the house. The phone is always busy, or else someone is screaming and you can't hear anyway.

Oh, Friday night was a disaster. Actually, there's sort of a disaster almost every day, but this one was really too much. I mean, I felt so bad for Esti. Esti and Eli are twins, and they do everything together. They're five. So, anyhow, Esti was carrying in this platter of some kind of beef that smelled yummy, with gravy and everything. She must have tripped or something, but she fell and dropped the whole thing. The meat slid onto the floor, there was gravy and broken pieces of that platter all over the place. It was really awful. Some people got spattered and they jumped up like they'd been shot. Poor Esti was a total mess, screaming and trying to put it all back together again. I thought Chaya would lose it. I mean, she's sort of strict. But she just got up, went to Esti, took her in her lap, and kissed her. Yitz and Nissim, that's the seven-year-old, cleaned it up with paper towels, and Yitz kept saying, "No problem! It's fine, fine!" He's really low-key. But everyone was sort of uncomfortable, you know? And it got really quiet in the room, like people were thinking, "Now, what's for dinner?" I mean, we did have salad, but the meat was ruined. Then Chaya said to Esti, "Look, Esti, you've given us a *Shabbos* we'll never forget, because you were really trying to help. You were doing a big *mitzvah* for Mommy." (That's a kindness, in case you didn't know, like I didn't know either before I got here.) So she says, "People didn't come for the meat. They came for the company." And then everyone went, "Yeah, we don't care." And some people said they never eat meat anyhow. Actually, I did care, because that meat really smelled great and I was hungry.

When are you coming? I miss you so much. Have you seen Jason? Is Hilary still seeing Scott? Who's lifeguarding at the pool? Please tell me all the noooze! I love you!

Marne

Hi, Kim! I forgot to tell you, you can email me back. Nobody will read it. They are really into privacy, which in a way is weird, cuz the house is so packed full of people. Say hi to your sisters and everyone. Let me know when you are coming!

Marne reread her email. She had left out some things. Like the people who wandered in asking questions of Chaya or Yitz: "What does the Torah say about such a case?" Or they asked questions about ancient times and Bible characters, quite as if they were still alive, living next door. "Why did Abraham sit out in the sun looking for guests when he was just recovering from his circumcision?" "Why did Sarah deny having laughed?"

Yitz answered each question carefully, stroking his beard, smiling. People came to borrow books and CDs. "So, sit and have something to eat!" In a moment Chaya would bring out some slices of loaf cake or cookies and fruit. The women's eyes gleamed as they kissed Chaya good-bye. The men pumped Yitz's hand and clapped him on the back.

Friday, three men came clad all in black, with black hats and bushy beards that made them look old, though they were only in their twenties. They played with the children, then huddled with Yitz, talking in gravelly voices, and when it came time for dinner, they sat at the table and hummed, louder and louder, backing up the tune with hearty slaps to the tabletop. It was too strange. Chaya only laughed and handed out great platters of food. Yitz sang with them, and once he pointed to the photograph on the opposite wall, the Rebbe with the white beard, his hand raised as if in blessing, smiling down upon the people assembled here. The smile held Marne's gaze. Then abruptly she looked away, hearing in her mind her mother's sharp voice, "Don't let them indoctrinate you, Marne! You are your own person, after all."

Friday night, just after the candles were lit, Yitz called all the children to him. They lined up, Becca first, down to the baby in Chaya's arms. Yitz laid his hands upon each one of their heads, murmuring a blessing. "May God make you like Sarah, Rachel, Rebecca, and Leah. . . . May God make you like Ephraim and Menashe. May God grant you peace." Even the baby seemed to be wrapped in the peace of the moment. When it was over, Yitz smiled at Marne. "Good *Shabbos*!" he said, and everyone echoed, "Good *Shabbos*!" and Marne felt an ache in her chest, wishing she could feel her father's hands framing her face, blessing her, giving her peace.

With all the static on the line, Marne could hardly recognize her mother's voice.

"How are you?" she kept saying. "Is everything all right? What time is it there?"

"Nine o'clock."

"A.m. or p.m.?"

"P.m.," Marne said, her eyes roving around the small den. Chaya had summoned her to the telephone, pointing to Yitz's small office. "You can have some privacy in here," she'd said with a nod and a smile. Then she closed the door so that Marne could be alone. The portable air conditioner hummed. Marne felt first relief, then a clammy chill.

"Oh. It's twelve hours later here," her mother said in her quick, breathless way. "Nine in the morning."

"Are you having a good time?" She wanted to be transported to Paris with its glamour and its novelty. She wanted to hear about Paris, the boulevards, the shops, the people, the music. But her mother's voice sounded rushed, high-pitched, and she talked much too fast.

"Yes, very hectic. I hardly have a moment. Except we did go to the Tuileries and the Louvre. We're on a tight schedule. Jerome, he's the guy in charge, wants everything immediately, preferably yesterday." She chuckled.

"Just like home," Marne muttered. Her mom sounded nervous, or maybe the quick banter was from guilt for not taking Marne with her.

"What? I can't hear you very well. The static's terrible. How's the weather there?"

"Hot. Very hot. But it's okay. I like it hot." She wanted to talk about the mothers and daughters she saw walking along the shore together or lying on colorful beach towels, rubbing each other's backs with oil. Sometimes before dinner, she and Becca took the kids to play in the sand, and they waded in the water. Marne molded sand people and huge sand castles. The children were delighted, screaming their pleasure at her artistry. And that night they chattered about it all through dinner, and Chaya told Marne, "I guess you inherited your mother's artistic talent."

"Have you heard from Dad?" her mother asked, sounding cautious.

"We spoke day before yesterday," Marne said. Chaya had called him before *Shabbos* to assure him that everything was fine. "We are enjoying your daughter so much! She's such a help. The kids already love her. Especially Becca. She's constantly telling me the clever things that Marne says and does."

"Is he okay?" Mom asked.

"Oh, yes." There was no telling, because her father's conversation was clipped, his voice exuding the phony "good ole boy" tone he used when he talked about surfing. It was like he wanted to be seventeen again and almost thought he was. He had asked her repeatedly, "Have you made some new friends? The surfing must be, like, wow! I hear the stores at Waikiki are really cool."

She hated it when he talked like that.

"So, how are they treating you?" her father had asked.

"Fine. Just fine." It was true. They were nice to her, considerate and respectful. But still, she was a stranger here. She tried to fit in, but somehow she was always a little off. Like her clothes, her music, her books. Surely her thoughts were different, too.

Now her mother asked the same question. "How are they treating you?"

"Well, it's okay," Marne said with a heavy feeling in her chest. "But I'm not like them." She felt resentment ready to burst out. She would tell her mother the incidents, the odd comments and questions, the words she couldn't translate.

"They're so into having people over!" she exclaimed. "I mean, all the time!" Her voice rose. "There's only two bathrooms for ten of us. And guests! Sometimes I have to wait . . ." Mom would say she was getting hysterical. She tried to stop herself, but the words poured out. "I feel funny wearing shorts, as if I'm doing something wrong. But I'm not going to stop either! Why should I?"

"Well, *of course* you can wear shorts!" her mother exclaimed. "You're your own person. Always remember that, Marne," she lectured. "Don't let anyone rob you of your individuality. You are a creative person. You know who you are and what you want!"

"Yes, Mom," she said dutifully, thinking, *That's you, not me.* She wished she did know who she was and what she wanted. And she felt guilty, for there was the other side, like the feeling of *Shabbos,* the sudden quiet, the comfort, and the long, lazy afternoon with people singing and laughing and hugging the children.

"Think of this," Mom said, "as a learning experience." She paused, then said breathlessly, "Hey, this call will cost a fortune. And I have to run over to the shop. Let's be sure and talk again in a few days. Do you need anything?"

"No, thanks. I have everything I need," Marne said. "My cell phone is broken," she said, an afterthought.

"Oh? That's too bad, honey. Maybe Itch will help you get it fixed."

"Yitz."

"What? Listen, sweetheart, I've really got to run. I love you!"

"Love you, too!" Marne chirped. And then the line went dead, and Marne sat down in Yitz's large leather chair. She closed her eyes, breathing deeply, feeling the cool, soft leather surrounding her body.

Hawaii. She ought to be enthralled. She was, after all, spending the summer in paradise. Incidents converged in her thoughts. Little Yossi screaming that Marne had to say a blessing before she took a drink of water. Becca and her *negel vasser* every morning. The kids at day camp singing about *Moshiach,* the Messiah, for whom they did not want to wait any longer. What did six-year-olds know about such things? In fact, what did she?

Nissim, digging into her suitcase one day, came upon the picture book, *Outside Over There.* He had asked her to read it to him.

"No," Marne said, her heart pounding.

"Why not? Isn't it appropriate?"

She had no answer. "I don't feel like it," she said.

"I can read it myself," he declared, dangling the book from his hand.

"No! Leave it alone!" She had almost shouted, and he retreated, hurt.

Now a lyric flowed into her mind, pure as trickling water.

> *Where can I go*
> *That I'll forget you?*
> *I'll never get you*
> *Out of my heart . . .*

She would play it, she decided, in a minor key.

Marne sat on the floor, her back against the bed. She strummed a few chords over and over again. "Mind if I play?"

"No, I love it," said Becca.

"Let me know when you want to go to sleep, and I'll quit."

"I don't sleep," Becca said.

"Sure you do."

"I don't sleep much," she said. "Sometimes I'm awake for hours."

"I didn't know that," Marne said. She played a C minor chord, then an A minor to F major. She sang softly, "How do I get you out of my heart?" She amended the last chord, played it again.

"That's beautiful," Becca said. She was propped up on one elbow, facing Marne. "Did you make that up?"

"I'm working on it," Marne said.

"It must be great to have a talent," Becca said. She chuckled. "I just have a talent for collecting junk."

Marne tightened one of the strings, strummed again, then said, "You could make something with all that metal stuff. A junk sculpture. I've seen those in a museum. They're neat."

"Really?" Becca seemed astonished. "Would you help me?"

"Sure."

"Marne," Becca said, her tone serious, "when you go out in the morning . . . ?"

"Yes? What about it?" Marne played several A minor seventh chords.

"And you're wearing those running shorts? I mean, do boys—do they look at you?"

"I don't know. I guess so. But I'm running, so . . ."

"Don't they try to—you know, whistle and stuff? Pick you up?"

Marne put the guitar down on her knees. "Pick me up? No, of course not. I'm just by myself, running. Did you think . . . ? What did you think?"

Becca put her head down. Her face was flushed. "I know you don't do anything wrong. But we read about Dinah, and how she went out and . . . well, she got raped."

Marne's eyes widened. "Who is Dinah?"

"In the Torah. She's Jacob's daughter. Went out to see the daughters of the land—that is, they weren't Jewish girls. They were, you know, pagan. And this guy saw her. He was the son of the king. And he took her and raped her. Because she didn't stay home and act modest."

Marne took in a deep breath, exhaled slowly. "I see. So, you think I'm going to get raped because I run? Because I wear shorts?"

"No, no," Becca said hastily, pushing back her hair, looking flustered. "I just wondered what happens . . ."

"Nothing happens!" Marne said, feeling exasperated. "I just run. Maybe people look at me. So what? I look at people, too. It doesn't mean anything."

"Okay, okay," said Becca. She turned away, hunched up under her sheet.

Marne put her guitar back in the case. She stood for a long moment, thinking, then she went to Becca's bed and sat down carefully. "Becca," she said, her hand on the small shoulder. "What's wrong?" Somehow she knew, by the rigid posture and the fitful breathing, that Becca was crying.

"Nothing," Becca piped.

"What's wrong?" Marne said again. She could feel the warmth of Becca's body. It drew her back, back to many years ago, when Jody came into her bed and they watched TV on that small set until Jody fell asleep. When Mom took Jody out to her own bed, there was still that warm indentation. She asked, "Are you afraid of—of boys?"

There was a long silence. Then Becca whispered in a high voice, "I guess so." She paused. "I didn't mean to hurt your feelings. I didn't say you do bad things."

"Look, some boys are mean," Marne said. "But some are nice. Like your father and your brothers. Jonathan and Nissim—don't you know other boys like them?"

"Yes, but . . ." Becca turned around, her eyes fastened upon Marne, as if she were searching out some truth. "When they do it—I mean, the rape, isn't it like when—I mean, when you get married? And make babies? Isn't it the same?"

Marne thought for a long moment. Then she said, "Becca, I'm not exactly sure of those things. I'm still— that is, you know, I'm only fifteen. But my mom told me it's very different. Rape is, well, someone getting into you by force. It's mean. It's awful, because you don't want it. Like, if someone breaks into your house and steals your food, it's very different from inviting them, isn't it?"

Becca nodded. "Yes," she breathed. "I guess so."

"So, when you love someone I guess you want to get close. You want to kiss them and make a baby because you love them so much. And then"—Marne remembered her mom's words—"it feels good. Like a hug. Only better."

"That's sex," Becca said stoutly, sitting up straight.

"Yeah," Marne said. "I guess."

Marne got into bed and switched out the light. A small night-light shone from across the room. And Marne realized that Becca was not only afraid of boys, but afraid of the dark, and afraid of leaving home. She had asked her just yesterday, "Will you be going away to school, like

76

Jonathan and Niss?" And Becca shook her head vehemently. "No! I don't have to go. Mom teaches me, and I have tapes. I don't have to go."

Now Marne whispered, "Maybe after I get back home, you could come and visit."

"Really?" Becca's voice sounded far away.

"My folks would take us places. Disneyland and Universal Studios. You could see how they make movies."

"Really? I love movies!" She sighed. "I wish you didn't have to go back. I wish you could stay here."

Marne's heart leaped. "Why?" She tensed, waiting.

"You're the only one who understands me," Becca said softly. Her voice was solemn, "Maybe your mom will let you stay. Don't you want to?"

"We'll see," Marne said, prevaricating. She thought of all the times she had asked questions of her parents, and when they were stuck they replied, "We'll see."

chapter SIX

Cranky and whining, soggy and pitiful, Bennie was teething, running a fever. He had to stay home with his mom while everyone else went to the airport to meet Jonathan. Marne had never seen such preparation, as if for a triumphant hero.

Nissim spent several days creating an enormous banner with poster paints on a ten-foot-long roll of white paper. WELCOME HOME, JONATHAN, the banner declared. It was decorated with balloons and little handprints, stars, and lots of glitter. Nissim enlisted Becca and Marne to hold up the banner, as they were the tallest among them, except for Yitz, who would be busy seeing about luggage and keeping the twins and Yossi out of trouble. The three youngest each had a helium balloon tied to their wrists, saying HURRAH! and WELCOME HOME! and WE LOVE YOU!

Preparations for Jonathan's homecoming almost exceeded those for *Shabbos*, but not quite. Yossi organized the toys, picking up stray game pieces and stacking all the

78

boxes on the family room buffet. Nissim came down from the upper bunk; that now belonged to Jonathan. Becca made chocolate chip cookies. Chaya baked a brisket with roasted onions and potatoes, Jonathan's favorite, and pineapple cake for dessert. Esti made place cards for the table, as if they might, in their excitement, actually forget their usual places. Of course, Jonathan would sit at his father's right hand, being the eldest, and Marne, as guest, sat at his left. She would be directly opposite Jonathan, listening to his stories, all the adventures that Nissim touted to her daily, marking off his calendar until the date circled in red actually arrived.

They got to the airport almost an hour ahead of time.

Nearly two weeks ago, Marne realized, she had stood at this very place, waiting for Chaya, expecting—what? Paradise, of course. Now she looked around at the girls in their short shorts and tank tops, the women wearing sundresses with thin spaghetti straps, the men without shirts, their bronze chests gleaming with sweat, and she wondered what Becca was thinking. But Becca, dressed in her long denim skirt and navy blue shirt, seemed oblivious to all the naked flesh, and to the intense heat.

It irritated Marne that they were so bundled up. What were they trying to prove? She edged away from Becca,

Yitz, and the kids, an observer, watching for glances of suspicion or malice. But nobody seemed to notice Yitz with his long beard and dark suit or Nissim and Elias with their *tzitzis,* or else they just didn't care.

How was it possible that nobody cared, when she was burning with embarrassment? Somehow they made her feel wrong, feel as if she had to explain and apologize for something she didn't believe in and didn't care about. Because they accused her in their nonconfrontational way, with their silent looks, for being what they called secular, not Jewish enough, not wearing tradition like a sign on her forehead. She clamped her teeth together, looking about, thinking, *There are probably plenty of Jews here, Jews like me who don't have to parade it around. Except, how can I tell who is and who isn't?* Ah, there was a man with his wife and two kids; the wife wore a small gold star around her neck, along with several other charms. She was screaming at her two boys. The man was dressed like a flashy gambler, his shirt open halfway down his chest, revealing a thick gold chain. He was shouting into a cell phone about some deal. "Put in an order!" he shouted. "Get with it, Clyde!" Embarrassing, Marne thought, squirming. But why should she care? She wondered whether Catholics did that, or Hindus. Were they always looking around for their coreligionists and wondering what people were thinking?

Marne went to the water fountain, let the cool water flow over her hands, over her wrists. She dampened her face and the back of her neck, feeling the flush of shame. She knew better than to label people. At camp they had sung songs about "one world" and "God loves everybody, even you and me!" She bit her lip, vexed at her own shallowness.

Now the man had put his cell phone away, and the woman had her two boys in tow. They walked with their arms around one another, laughing. And Marne realized that she was jealous. Her parents never walked with their arms around each other. When did they ever even walk side by side?

"Come on, come on, Marne!" Nissim shouted, and ran to Marne, his *tzitzis* swinging wildly, arms waving. "The plane—look, it's coming! Hold up the sign. Get Becca. Hurry!"

Into the flurry of excited greeters they went, Esti squealing, Elias tugging at his dad, Nissim directing Marne and Becca, "Hold it higher! Higher! Get on your tippy-toes."

There were the usual happy cries, the flower leis and

kisses, as one after another the people tumbled out, astonished at the warmth and the fragrance that embraced them. And Marne remembered the first touch of those trade winds, the first whiff of Hawaiian flowers. It was an elixir.

There was no mistaking Jonathan. He was smaller than Marne had imagined, dressed in a black suit, the jacket open to reveal a crumpled white dress shirt. But most preposterous was that hat, a replica of the broad-brimmed black hat his father wore, making him look like a little kid dressed up in his father's clothes. His expression was sober, almost troubled, as if he were worrying about his luggage and other weighty matters. He carried a leather bag, similar to a briefcase, while behind him an exuberant group of teenagers came running with their sneakers and backpacks, beeping into their cell phones, earphones dangling over their chests.

Jonathan had landed, it seemed, from a different world.

"Jonathan!" Nissim screamed. He ran, throwing himself upon his brother, delivering a swift punch to Jonathan's chest. Jonathan doubled over, laughing, in mock pain.

"Hey, Niss, buddy—you've gotten so big! Wait till we get home. I think I can still take you down."

"Welcome home!" Becca called, shaking her end of

the banner. Marne's arms were tingling, but Becca would not set the banner down.

Now Esti and Elias encircled Jonathan, shrieking out their news of wading pools and new games and the nice or nasty kids at day camp.

Yitz stood back, holding Yossi in his arms, smiling his gentle smile. When the commotion waned, he strode over to Jonathan and put his hand on the boy's shoulder. "Good to see you, son."

Jonathan nodded, gazing up into his father's face. "Whew! A long trip."

"The car's right over there. Go get your luggage and we'll go home. Your mother is anxious to see you. Wait! Jonathan, this is your cousin Marne."

"Hi," Marne said, smiling. "Cousin," she added. "Until now, I haven't really known any cousins."

"Hi," Jonathan said brusquely, looking down, so that she saw the fullness of his eyebrows and the faint fuzz along the side of his face and jaw.

Without another word, he turned and hurried to the baggage carousel. "Is he always so talkative?" Marne asked Becca.

Becca shrugged. "Don't mind him. He doesn't often talk to girls."

"Not even to you?"

"Hardly." She flipped her hair back. "I don't care. He's weird. Like most boys."

At dinnertime the focus was on Jonathan. He was number one, top banana, first one at the washstand, first one served, dominating the conversation by answering his mother's unabated flow of questions. "And how is Grandma? And your aunt Phyllis? And the children?" She named them one after the other, and people she knew in Brooklyn, and shops she liked to visit, and the sandwich store, the candy store, the ice cream store, until Marne thought she would scream. Why didn't Chaya just take a trip to New York? What was so great about a bunch of stores?

"That's where we lived," Chaya explained with a glance at Marne; she might have read her mind. "When Yitz and I were first married. It's where Jonathan and Becca were born. We have friends there."

"I see," Marne said, and for a moment she did see how it must be for Chaya here on this island, without any friends from her school days, nobody to share the countless daily details of her life. Of course, the house was always full of people, and everyone was friendly. But a *friend*—that was different.

They hung Nissim's banner over the doorway, so that on the first *Shabbos* that Jonathan was back, everyone launched into the welcome mode, the women beaming and smiling endlessly, the men clapping Jonathan on the back, making small talk about the Yankees, the *yeshiva,* how much Jonathan had grown.

Old Shirley pinched Jonathan's cheeks. Marjorie stood in front of him, telling some story about her trip to Seattle. Sol praised him for being a *yeshiva* student, talked about his own student days, the long hours poring over books. "But it didn't hurt me none—so, you are a scholar!"

Jonathan answered everyone with that same serious look, his green eyes downcast, though he seemed to be hiding a slight smile. He enjoyed his role immensely.

At least that's how Marne saw it. Jonathan ignored her, except perhaps to say, "Please pass the orange soda." He was obviously addicted to orange soda and sat with a small orange mustache on his upper lip, mingling with the fuzz, until he remembered and wiped it carefully away. Silly kid. How could anyone be so different? So serious? It shocked Marne to realize that they were about the same age. She was just a few months older.

During the service in the living room on Friday night,

Jonathan stood beside his father, echoing his words, bobbing and swaying in prayer. And when Yitz began to sing, Jonathan's voice rang out. No longer shy or reticent, he threw back his head and sang as if he were reaching far beyond this room, these walls, this island. Marne, startled, soaked up the sound, the harmony, the beauty of their blended voices.

And then it was over, and Jonathan was just himself again, aloof and preoccupied.

Saturday—day of marathon prayer, Marne called it, watching with half-amused interest the intensity that infused every act with new meaning. No lights were turned on or off; a timer took care of that. No stove or burner was lit: Chaya kept the oven on low, with a huge pot of stew in it, and sometimes also a fruit pudding that was served warm. Marne had learned the hard way that if she wanted to wash her hair, she'd better do it before sundown on Friday—no bathing until Saturday night. And then there were the positive commands: clean clothes, modest behavior, quiet joy, companionship.

A number of people came back every week. They brought gifts of food or flowers, kissed the children. "I love it here," they said. "It's so peaceful."

"Rabbi, you are wonderful. The way you keep the traditions!" they said.

One woman always hugged Chaya and insisted on sitting beside her. "My grandparents kept kosher," she said. "When I walk in and smell that roasted chicken and *kishke,* I feel like I'm back home in the Bronx."

There were travelers looking for a meal, for solace, for information. Young couples on their way to Thailand or Bora-Bora, tourists from the mainland looking for a Sabbath service ended up here because there was no other service in town. Some never went to synagogue back home; it seemed like an interesting thing to do on vacation. They sat at the head of the table, usually right beside Yitz, and they often challenged him.

"I'm a good person, Rabbi. Why should my life be dominated by all these rules? Who can even prove that God exists? And how do you know what God wants from me?"

"The Torah," Yitz would say. "The blueprint for our existence."

"Look, all this ritual doesn't belong in the modern world, Rabbi. It was fine when the Jews were herded into ghettos and had no place else to go, nothing else to do. . . ."

"You don't even turn on TV? You don't drive on Saturday? Come on, Rabbi. They didn't have cars in biblical

87

times. What rules could possibly apply to our time? Things change."

"The rules don't change," came the reply. "The Torah is our instruction book. If we live by its laws, we survive. We prosper."

"Then how come people who follow all those rules also suffer?"

Yitz threw up his hands. "Ah, that is one of the greatest difficulties for us. We always assume that pain is punishment. Couldn't it be a vehicle toward growth?"

Questions flew. "Who really wrote the Torah?" "Was it Moses?" "Was it actually written by God?" "Did Moses only copy down what he was told?" "Did he make it up?"

"I think God inspired Moses to write it," Marne found herself saying, amazed that she even formed the thought. "When a person writes a song," she went on, her cheeks burning from her own boldness, "isn't it inspired? I imagine God has something to do with creativity."

Chaya gave her a broad smile. "It's a good question. How much comes from our own efforts, and how much from God?"

"I have no problem with any of this," said one man, slapping the table. "Moses was a great, charismatic leader.

Somehow he persuaded the people that all those commandments came from God." The man looked around at his audience. "Not too different from politicians today!"

That created another uproar, as people were launched from religion to politics. Kim would have had a fit, Marne thought. Discussions like this always left her bored, rolling her eyes and groaning. More and more lately Marne reflected on their friendship, how it had come about, how it was sustained. Marne answered herself. Kim was fun.

And she was generous. Kim never judged her either. With Kim, Marne could be quiet or talkative, excited or sad. She just wasn't deep, but so what?

At first *Shabbos* seemed eternally long, and Marne couldn't wait to turn on the TV or wash her hair or play the songs on her iPod. She pretended that she was at camp, and somehow as she surrendered to the *Shabbos* mode, things fell into place. She would play checkers or chess with Nissim or sing songs with Esti and Eli. After a while she would go into her room, take out her guitar, and play softly, rebelling inwardly against the rule about playing instruments on the Sabbath. It was perplexing. They said they loved music. Sabbath was a time for joy. What could be more joyful than making music?

89

No. Leave the world alone. Listen to the waves and the wind and the birds. Let it be the source of your joy. Marne's mind became filled with Chaya's and Yitz's pronouncements, and now even Jonathan occasionally gave her advice.

"Why don't you learn some Hebrew songs to play for the kids?" he suggested.

"Why don't they learn ordinary songs?" Marne argued. "Don't they need to live in the real world?"

" 'I've Been Working on the Railroad' is the real world?" Jonathan snapped. He crept away. If Yitz had heard this exchange, Marne knew, Jonathan would be in trouble.

Nobody ever corrected her overtly. It was considered too rude, inappropriate. Maybe that made it worse. There was nothing to respond to; it was all so subtle.

At least the kids at camp had no hidden agenda. They clustered around Marne as soon as she appeared, begging her to teach them songs. And she taught them all the old camp standards she knew. They laughed and clapped and danced around her. What they loved best were the silly songs she made up, asking them to help supply their own words:

Oh, the sea,
I see the sea,
do you see me?
I found a flea
attached to me.
How can it be?
Into the sea
I'll surely flee.
I see the sea.
Do you see me?

They laughed and clapped. They thought she was brilliant. The little girls came to hug Marne, and she hugged them back and showed them how to make things, beanbags and twirling mobiles from thread and wire hangers and bits of aluminum, spatter paintings and sand pictures.

"You are so creative!" Becca and Chaya praised her. "Where did you learn all this?"

Marne shrugged. "Different places, school and camp." It pleased her that they thought she had talent, and she believed it, until the first Saturday that Jonathan sang alone.

They had all eaten their lunch of salads and fish and Chaya's *cholent*. It was an unusually large crowd, nearly thirty people stuffed into the dining room, spilling out into the family room, sitting at tables, on cushions and sofas. Someone at the table started a song without words, a *niggun*, tapping its rhythm on the tabletop. Others joined in, the men singing loudly, like pirates on a ship, Marne thought, a little raucous and boastful, bodies swaying, heads thrown back in abandon. Several women joined in, Marjorie with her thin little voice, stout Shirley slapping her hands together, and three girls with long blond hair. They were about nineteen or twenty, best friends, Marne could tell, island-hopping on vacation and hunting for guys. Somehow they had ended up here on a lark, trying it out, coming for *Shabbos* the way travelers might explore underwater caves or witness a native dance spectacle.

Marne saw them whispering together. The girls signaled to each other with their eyes and body movements—a shrug, a lift of the brow. They were bonded in their fascination, their eyes glittering with their discovery, as if they had stumbled onto some exotic hidden society.

Marne, embarrassed, tried to make small talk with them at lunch. "Where're you from?" "Oregon—she's from Seattle." "Have you been to the big mall? Seen the perfume factory?" They would have none of it. The girls leaned toward Yitz, absorbing his actions as he sliced the *challah* with deliberate care, sprinkled it with salt, and passed a piece to everyone at the table. One of the girls shot out questions. Yitz replied, "The two *challahs* represent the double portion of manna that was provided for *Shabbos* when the Jews were in the desert. You see, on *Shabbos,* they were not allowed to gather it."

"Because gathering is work?" she questioned.

"Yes. There are thirty-nine actions that constitute *Shabbos* work—weaving, gathering, cooking . . ."

"Ah. Ummm . . . ," they murmured appreciatively.

"But you can move your piano to another room if you want!" Nissim declared loudly, and everyone laughed while Yitz nodded his approval.

Old Sol started a song in his deep, crackling voice. *"Da-da-da-dee-dee-tum."* Others joined in. The three girls picked up the tune, laughing and swaying. The men sang louder still, until the room was rocking with sound, and even Esti and Elias, usually subdued when there was company, stood up and danced around the table, waving their hands and giggling.

Out of the cacophony came a single note, a separate note, gradually rising above the rest. It held. Separated from all the others, deep and pure, the one note split into two, and then a third. Each note seemed to vibrate with meaning, blending into the next, the syllables now clearly ringing, *"Ri-bo-no . . ."* on and on, the timbre increasing, the three notes expanding into a higher key, *"Ri-bo-no . . . Ribono shel olam! Ribono shel olam!"* Jonathan seemed utterly involved in the song that burst from his mouth, his eyes half closed, his voice rising in fervor. Jonathan had lost all sense of self; he was transported, as Marne felt transported when she ran her hardest and her best, arriving at last with that feeling of awe and exaltation. The song simply flowed, carrying Jonathan with it. *"Ri-bo-no shel olam, ri-bo-no shel olam!"* It filled the air. It pressed into the walls, stretched up to the ceiling. The music carried everyone along in its power, pure as a river, amazing as a waterfall. *"Ribono shel olammmm!"* Nobody moved. All were locked together, listening. *"Ri-bo-no she-el olam! Ribono she-el olam, ribono shel olam!"*

Marne's throat tightened. Tears filled her eyes. Her skin felt too tender. The song lifted her up, raised her high, beyond words, then flung her down again as it abruptly ceased. The silence held for a long moment. Then came applause.

Voices, like sudden scattered bits of hail, broke the spell. "Did he compose that? Where did he *find* that?"

"He's always singing. It's his talent."

"What does it mean? *Ribono . . .*"

"Master. Master of the universe. It's like a mantra."

"Ah, a mantra," said one of the young blondes from Oregon. "Far-out. Like India."

Across the table, Marne met Becca's eyes. Their gaze held a shared awareness that Jonathan, aloof and introspective Jonathan, had traveled far beyond anyone in this room.

chapter SEVEN

Kim,

You won't believe what happened. I was jogging as usual, along that same stretch of beach—oh, it's so gorgeous in the morning just after the sun comes up. I can't wait until you get here and we can jog together. Anyhow, I was jogging by and those cute boys were there—that is, two of them, and one went straight into the surf, but the other one, Jeff, was just standing there waiting for something. Waiting for me, as he told me later. He'd been watching me every morning, he said. This time he yelled, "Hey! You're really racing! I clocked you from the lifeguard tower to here—it's exactly one mile. Seven minutes, twenty-three seconds. Not bad!"

Well, of course I stopped, and we talked. He is so cute! He didn't look shy or dumb, you know how some guys get when they talk to you, sort of looking away. He looked right at me the whole time, but he didn't make me feel self-conscious at all. He's from San Diego, but he's been living in Hawaii for the past three years. His dad's stationed here. So of course we started talking all about California and what it's like living on the Island. That's what they call it here, the Island. It's really neat, Jeff says, because he gets to surf every day and doesn't have to wear shoes half the time. It's really casual. But there's hardly any haole girls for him to hang out with, so he gets pretty bored. Haoles, in case you didn't know, are us, white folks from the mainland. When people live here, even haoles, they get a discount from all the stores. You just tell them you're a *kama'aina,* and you get a discount. Jeff said when he first saw me he thought I was a regular tourist, but now he could tell I'm staying here. He said he saw me last week taking Nissim for ice cream at that little strip mall. He thought Nissim was my little brother— same color hair. He said he really wanted to talk to me, but he didn't want to seem forward. But he said he recognized me from the beach, because he saw that I was a fabulous runner! Then he looked down and sort of blushed. It was so cute! He's got a gorgeous tan, and great shoulders, muscles from surfing. Wow! And then I told him, "Well, I noticed you, too, because you're here every morning with your friends. But you're always looking out at the surf. So I thought . . ." So then he said he'd been watching for me every morning, and he wondered why I didn't show up on Saturday. He was worried I'd gone back to the mainland, he said. So we started talking about everything, his school, his dad, how he misses San Diego, even though Hawaii is supposed to be paradise. He told me that after a while people get island fever, and they have to get off. Isn't that wild? I mean, you'd think this would be the best place in the world, with the trade winds and the flowers and the music. Well, we talked for over an hour, and he walked me back to the house. When we got there, Chaya was piling all the kids into the car for day camp, and she was just furious. I mean, she looked at me as if I was a criminal! It was so embarrassing. But I held my ground. I went, "Aunt Chaya, I'd like you to meet my friend Jeff. He's originally from San Diego."

So Chaya goes, "Pleased to meetcha," really quick, and she shoos the kids into the car and tells me Yitz will drive me to the day camp hut so I can play my guitar for the kids and help them make collages. She tells me I promised. I did no such thing! How could she do that to me? So Jeff just says he'd better go and maybe he'll see me later. I swear, I was so embarrassed! I'm sitting there wanting to scream!!!

I can't wait until you get here. Jeff has these two adorable surfer friends. We'll hang out together! If you weren't coming here, I'd go back home, I swear. I'm starting to feel stifled! Maybe it's island fever???

Love you! Don't forget my flip-flops!

Marne

That night, after the kids were in bed, Chaya came to her, as if they shared a secret. "Come on into the kitchen," she whispered. "I made us some cocoa."

"What about Becca?"

"She doesn't drink cocoa," Chaya whispered. "Anyhow, she's fast asleep."

"She told me she never sleeps," Marne muttered.

"Shh! Come on. Just us. Yitz is at a meeting."

They sat at the kitchen table. Chaya popped a marshmallow into Marne's cup, and it began to melt, just the way Marne liked it.

"I'm sorry if I embarrassed you this morning," Chaya said, her eyes intent on Marne's face. "It's a terrible thing to do to a person."

"It's okay," Marne said tonelessly. She looked away.

"No. Really. We learn that there is no place in the world to come for someone who embarrasses another person in public."

Marne smiled slightly. "It wasn't exactly public. Just us."

"Well, thank you for not being angry."

"I was angry," Marne said, surprised that somehow the anger had dissipated. "I'm old enough to talk to a boy. I wasn't doing anything wrong."

"I was just worried. Frantic, actually, when you didn't come home. I imagined—all sorts of things. I suppose I'm silly, feeling so responsible. But I . . ."

"It's okay," Marne said. "I'm just not used to . . ."

"Does your mother let you date?"

"Date? Yeah. I guess. I go out with my friends. Some of them are boys. My mother doesn't see anything wrong with that."

"You are fifteen," she said, emphasizing *fifteen*. Then she asked, leaning toward Marne, "Where do you go? Do you go to movies? Dancing?"

"We go to the movies. We go to the mall. We play tennis or hang out at the beach." Marne felt the heat rising to her face. She pushed her cocoa aside. Annoyance drummed inside her, threatening to explode into anger. "I'm not afraid of boys," she went on. "All my friends date. It doesn't mean that we—"

"Look, I'm not criticizing you or your mother," Chaya said.

"Then why are we talking about this?" Marne cried.

Chaya sipped her cocoa, wiped her mouth carefully with a napkin. "You're away from home, Marne. I just want to do the right thing. So many things can happen to a girl."

"You're implying I'll get raped," Marne said coldly. "Like Dinah."

Chaya looked startled. She sighed. "I don't mean that at all."

"Excuse me, but my mom thinks you're living in the

Dark Ages. She doesn't mind if I go out with boys. How can I ever get to know boys if I never talk to them? How can I ever be ready for marriage and all that stuff?"

Chaya smiled. "Well, there are ways. Other ways."

"Really?" Marne stood up, pushing her hair back, exasperated. "I can't imagine how you get to know someone without talking to them!"

Chaya rose and walked to the counter, picked up a napkin, and wiped her brow. She came back to the table, sat down, and leaned toward Marne, a determined look in her eyes. "You are important to me, Marne. You're family. More than that, you're one of us, a Jew." She smiled. "We used to say 'a member of the tribe.' Have you ever heard that expression?"

"No," Marne said irritably. She didn't want to be in a tribe. She didn't want this entire discussion. But since Chaya had started it, she wasn't about to retreat. "I think the main thing is that all people are created equal. Isn't that so? Aren't we all the same in God's eyes?"

"The same," Chaya said, "but also different." She looked triumphant, as if she'd been waiting for just this argument. "God created all the animals, but you can't claim that a giraffe is the same as a lion. Each has a different purpose and different ways of fulfilling that purpose. Jews have the Torah. That's what God gave us, and the way we fulfill it is to teach it to our children. If we marry Jews, our children will carry on the tradition. It's that simple—and that difficult. Because there are so many temptations."

"If Judaism is so great," Marne argued, feeling her temper rise, "why are we so tempted?"

Now Marne saw the struggle in Chaya's face, her flushed cheeks, the darkness of her pupils. Marne felt that she was on the verge of something brilliant, something certain.

At last Chaya said, "We all face temptations. We have two sides in us, the good inclination and the evil inclination. It's up to us to choose which one wins in any situation."

"Maybe my good inclination makes me reach out to other people," Marne argued. "To non-Jews."

"Maybe," Chaya said, nodding slowly. "Marne, I know that our values are different. Ours seems like a difficult life. But . . ." She shook her head. "I think it's what we are meant to do. It feels—right. And the Torah tells us it *is* right."

"So," Marne said stubbornly, "it gets down to whether you believe the Torah was written by God. Whether it really is what Yitz calls the blueprint for our existence."

"Exactly," said Chaya. She rose and put her hand on Marne's shoulder. Marne did not turn. She allowed the touch without moving or making any reciprocal gesture that might indicate that she was convinced.

When Chaya left, Marne stepped outside. She stood at the edge of the patio, where the asphalt met the sand. Masses of stars were collected above her, and she recalled the admonition in the prayer book that God is incorporeal, without any attributes that we can perceive. And yet, the sages insisted, He is there. If we do not reach Him, it is not His fault, but ours.

"Then give me a sign," Marne whispered petulantly. "Anything. A shooting star or a bird landing right here at my feet. That wouldn't be too difficult, would it? I'm not asking for a fig tree to sprout or a lion to come out of the ocean. Just something ordinary."

Marne stood, hands braced against her sides, waiting.

Marne pulled her hair back into a ponytail and tied it with a bright red-and-pink scarf that trailed down her back. A little lipstick and a touch of mascara made her feel good. She ran out, imagining what she would say to Jeff, how he might respond. They'd sit in the sand and watch the waves, talk and talk and talk.

But neither Jeff nor his friends were there. She felt the ache of disappointment. She hadn't realized how much she looked forward to seeing Jeff. She felt strongly the irony of being surrounded by people yet alone, being in paradise but longing for someone to share it, someone like her. Someone exactly like Jeff.

Twice Marne took the bus to Waikiki, and once Chaya drove her there, so that she could try to satisfy her restlessness by going in and out of the shops, trying on trinkets, watching all the beautiful women in their shorts and sundresses, their long hair and flashing fingernails. She felt plain and dissatisfied, counting the days until Kim would come and rescue her.

One late afternoon she sat alone on her bed, surrounded by the scent of blossoms from the pikake tree outside the window. Lavender shadows poured into the room, bringing a graceful, storybook aura. Marne reached deep into her suitcase and took out the book. She gazed at the cover with its elaborate artwork; she opened the pages, saw the arbor, Flora the beautiful, fairy-tale girl, the goblins who came to steal the baby away. Marne sat with the book on her lap, reliving that night, gazing at the pictures as if she had never seen them before. And a feeling descended upon her, a strange tranquillity, deep sorrow mixed with a distant hope, the certainty that somehow, somewhere, Jody lived. Eventually, they would find each other, just like in the story.

She recalled the therapist's comments. His name was Avery, and he had a way of staring at her without blinking, as if by his gaze he could absorb her, transform her thoughts, and make her whole.

"It's not unusual," Avery had said, "for people to attach to some substance or symbol after a trauma. Some people use drugs. Others find compulsions, like continually checking the stove or washing their hands. It's a release from stress."

Marne only nodded. Was she expected to answer? She felt like a broken clock or a faulty computer, designed to function but now, somehow, gone wrong. And here was the fixer, the shrink. One new set of wires or attachments, and she'd be as good as new.

"That book is pretty scary, isn't it?" Avery had said in a tone that suggested they were on the same team. Pals. "What age kid do you think would be scared by that story?"

Marne knew exactly what he was getting at. She was much too old to be taken in by fairy tales. But she knew about symbols and metaphors from that special reading class last summer. The book was really about evil, about being suddenly attacked without cause. It was about anger and fear and confusion. In the book, the end brought resolution. Life returned to normal. "It doesn't scare me," Marne had said. Boldly she met the therapist's gaze. "The goblins brought the baby home. They brought her back."

"And you think Jody's going to come back? That whoever took her will bring her back?"

"It's possible."

"Yes." The therapist sighed. He glanced at Marne's mom, then back at her. "Of course. It's possible. We have to stay positive."

Later she heard him telling Mom, "Give her time. It takes time."

Nissim burst into the room. "Becca! Becca, have you seen my—" He stopped and looked at Marne. "What are you reading?"

Hastily, Marne slipped the book under her blanket. But Nissim had seen. "I know that story," he said. "We got it from the library."

"Good for you."

"Will you read it to me?"

Marne paused. Nissim sat down on the floor, his back against the bed, and turned to look at her expectantly.

"Okay," she said with a sigh. "Why not?"

She read the story slowly, letting herself be drawn into it, feeling Nissim's rapt involvement.

When it was over he said, "I like that story."

"I like it, too," said Marne.

"Why did they steal the baby?" he asked, frowning. "Why would anyone be so mean?"

"I don't know," Marne said, tucking the book back into her suitcase. "I guess there are some bad people around."

"That's true," Nissim said solemnly. "Like, in the morning prayers, we ask *Hashem* to keep them away from us."

"Does it work?" said Marne.

"I had a fight once," Nissim said. "This kid started punching me. I got a black eye."

"Did you fight back?"

"I punched him hard as I could. Also, I kicked him. You know where."

"Good for you!" Marne laughed.

"Jonathan told me *yeshiva* isn't so bad," Nissim offered. "He says they get to go places, like Rockefeller Center. They went and saw the Statue of Liberty."

"You might like it," said Marne. "Tell me, what are those things your father wears on his head?"

"A *kippa*?"

"No. In the morning, those boxes and straps."

"*Tefillin*."

"Oh. Thanks. Okay. What's inside the boxes?"

"Prayers."

"He *wears* them?"

"Yeah."

"Do you have them, too?"

"No. Jonathan does. You have to be a *bar mitzvah*. Thirteen. I'm only seven."

She had seen Yitz in his den that morning, brown leather straps wound around his head and his left arm. Straps across his forehead held a small brown box. He was bent over his prayer book, swaying back and forth.

She had slipped away quickly, embarrassed.

She hoped her dad would call. She wondered, did he know about this? Maybe he knew about morning prayers and Sabbath candles and not turning on the TV or the stove on Saturday. She had never asked him about any of those things, like where God is, or what He wanted people to do, or why He let Jody be kidnapped.

The word was like a stone in her throat. She never said it, even to herself. Now she whispered the words. "My little sister was kidnapped."

"I know," Nissim whispered back. He looked down at the floor. "My mom told us."

"She did?"

"We pray for her."

"That she'll be found?"

He shrugged. "That wherever she is, she is okay. She's fine."

"Thanks," Marne whispered.

Later that evening she found Yitz outside, looking up at the stars, an empty garbage can beside him. "Hi, Marne! I was just doing my job." He chuckled. "I used to hate taking out the trash. Now, every time, I stay out for a while and look at the sky. It's so beautiful here. Not like Brooklyn." He chuckled again. "Of course, Brooklyn has its points."

"Why did you leave? Aren't all your friends there?"

"We came here because it's where the Rebbe needs us to be," he said simply.

She said, "Tell me about *tefillin*. What's inside those

boxes?" Here in the darkness, she didn't feel so shy or reluctant.

"Prayers," Yitz said. "Prayers about the oneness of God. It is the main principle of our faith. Do you know the *Shema*?"

"Yes." Marne felt her face becoming warm. "I went to Sunday school for a while," she said. "The kids were so wild and it was so boring, Mom let me quit. Dad never did care. His parents never made him go to Sunday school or anything. He says religion is just a crutch."

"Hmm. Yes," Yitz said. "I know people say that. I suppose, in a way, it is. It helps people walk straight."

"They kept telling us about the holidays. We did stupid crafts."

"But they didn't teach you about *tefillin*," Yitz said with a nod. "Well, this is what Jewish men do every morning. Put on these prayer boxes and say the morning prayers."

"My father doesn't."

"Observant Jewish men," he corrected.

"What about women?"

"They don't have to do it. Women have other duties."

"What about a career?"

Yitz smiled, his teeth showing white in the moonlight.

"Sure, that's fine. My friend's wife has five kids. She's also a nurse."

"Can a woman do *tefillin*?"

Yitz paused. Then he said, "Some women have been known to wear *tefillin*. Some famous women, in fact."

She followed his gaze to the stars. "Thanks for telling me."

"No problem."

And Marne dreamed that night of standing in the yard, looking at the stars, flying up to meet them, then falling, hard, onto the earth. She awakened with a start, hearing the sound of water trickling into a bowl. *Negel vasser,* she thought, shaking her head.

She glanced at the wall calendar. Kim was coming in eight more days. She could hardly wait.

chapter EIGHT

It was stifling in the large kitchen, with spaghetti steaming on the stove and several pans of cookies in the oven. By now Marne could tell from the humidity that rain was imminent. Then the downpour would crackle against the house; rain would swish and stream from the gutters. Soon the sun would glow again, with warm mist rising from the pavement, giving off that after-rain smell. The dark green leaves of the pikake tree would be washed bright and clean.

Marne sat on the old sofa, bits of cotton wedged between her toes, bright red polish in her hand. From the CD player came the ebullient sounds of Uncle Moishy singing in Yiddish. The twins twirled and stomped, oblivious to the heat. "Esti!" Marne finally called. "Sit down here, and I'll paint your toenails when I'm done."

"Why are you doing that?" Jonathan looked up from his magazine. "Who sees your toes?"

"Don't be rude, Jonathan," snapped Chaya, straightening up after wiping orange juice off the floor.

"Neat!" screamed Esti. She jumped up on the sofa. Marne clutched the bottle of polish until the uproar had subsided.

The phone rang. "Get it, please, Becca!" Chaya was dragging a sack of potatoes off to the pantry.

Becca grabbed the phone, poised like her mother, with the receiver clutched under her chin.

"I'm sorry," she said. "Rabbi left for Maui this morning. He's doing a wedding." Becca paused. "Two days, I think."

She turned to her mother. "When's Dad coming back?"

"Thursday. Late afternoon. Who's on the phone, Becca?"

"I don't know. Someone needs a burial."

Chaya reached over and grabbed the phone. "Hello? Yes, of course we do." She held Bennie on one hip, juggling the phone, trying to keep the baby from pulling her beads, brown Hawaiian pods interspersed with pink shells.

"When did she die?" Chaya frowned. "Oh, yes. Absolutely. As soon as possible." She shot a look at the clock, tucked the telephone under her chin, flipped through her calendar, a thick, battered black notebook.

"It should be today," she said decisively.

Marne looked at Becca, mouthing the words, "What's going on?"

Becca only shrugged.

"I can get there in an hour," Chaya said. "She's at the funeral home? Good. Do you have a plain white cotton sheet? Fine. No, don't worry. I'll bring everything we need. Just a clean cotton sheet. No. We won't need that. You said she wanted an Orthodox burial. Traditional, we call it. Have you picked out a casket? All right. Good. I'll be glad to. Meanwhile, you can call the airline and make the arrangements. About two hours. Barring unforeseen circumstances."

Marne saw that Chaya's face was damp with sweat. Unceremoniously she handed the baby to Becca, who immediately jostled him on her hip, puffing out her lips in a soft raspberry.

Chaya hung up, hands clasped, eyes casting about, obviously in managerial mode. By now, Marne knew that look. It reminded Marne of her mother, those sudden spurts of energy just before she left for work. Sometimes Marne caught a fleeting glimpse of her mom in a certain expression on Aunt Chaya's face. It was always startling.

Chaya pulled the trays of cookies out of the oven. "Becca, if I don't get back, just fix the spaghetti for dinner.

Jonathan, go check my *taharah* box in the garage. Be sure there are three buckets, gloves . . ."

She glanced at Marne. "Would you mind making a few sandwiches? We'll need six, at least. There's bread in the box, some cold cuts in the fridge."

"Do you want cheese?" Marne asked.

"No!" Becca and Chaya both exclaimed.

Marne bit her lip. She kept on forgetting that they never ate meat and dairy at the same meal. Jonathan had given her a long-winded explanation about boiling a calf in its mother's milk, but it didn't make sense, though Marne tried to appear convinced, just to get him to stop. Now she padded across the kitchen, Esti pulling at her shirttail. "You said you'd polish my toenails! You said!"

"I will," Marne said, "later. You want to help me make sandwiches?"

"Goodie! I'll do the mayonnaise." She rushed to the refrigerator and took out a large jar. Marne caught it just in time. She took out the wheat bread and lined up the slices on the counter, wondering why, for a burial, sandwiches were needed. She didn't dare to ask, for Chaya was poring through her address book, punching in numbers, frowning as she spoke.

"Janie? I need your help. A burial. Today." A pause,

then Chaya grunted, "Oh, no! Can't you postpone . . . ? Oh. I see." She punched in another number and began speaking in her rapid way, English interspersed with phrases Marne didn't comprehend. "Yes, *baruch Hashem* . . . everyone's fine. I hope you're available for a *taharah*. . . ."

Marne made the sandwiches, standing on one foot, protecting her polish job. She let Esti spread the mayonnaise and Elias slap on the mustard, feeling virtuous for her patience. Marne put on the meat and a piece of lettuce, wondering if Chaya wanted them cut in halves or quarters. Did it matter? Small things seemed to be imbued with significance here. Did she want the crusts cut off? Jody always wanted the crusts removed. She ate them last, chewing and chewing. *Funny,* Marne thought, *the things you remember.*

Chaya banged down the receiver. "Gloria's gone off to Chicago. Her daughter's about to give birth. Nadine is in bed with a bad cold. Frances didn't answer. Probably went to the mainland. We should have four. Well, at least Kalima said she'll come. Dear, faithful Kalima."

Chaya's eyes roved around the room. "We should have four," she repeated thoughtfully. "It's recommended. Two can do it, but still . . ."

Becca moved across the room, taking the baby with her. "Don't look at me," she muttered.

"I need you to take care of Yossi and the baby," Chaya said, looking distracted. "Jonathan will play with the twins, won't you, Jonathan? And help Nissim with his model."

He looked up, nodding. "Sure. We'll go out and play soccer."

"That's my boy!" Chaya's gaze fastened on Marne.

Marne wrapped the sandwiches and snapped open a paper bag, feeling efficient.

"Marne," Chaya said slowly, "I need to talk to you."

"All right," said Marne. Something in the way Chaya looked at her projected a warning.

"Come into the den," Chaya said, leading the way.

Marne followed. The den was cool. A portable air conditioner was tucked into the window, offering relief, then a chill. "It's cold in here," Marne said.

"Yitz can't stand heat."

"Then why'd he move to Hawaii?"

"His work. For the Rebbe," Chaya said, indicating the photograph on the wall. "Look, Marne, I have to ask you something." Chaya moistened her lips, her eyes flicking sideways, then back to focus fully on Marne. "I need help. First of all, do you have your period?"

"What? You mean, now?"

"Now. Because if you do . . ."

"No. I don't."

"Good. That is, Marne, I have to go and do a burial. That is, not a burial, but the preparation. This woman— she was not religious, but she asked for a traditional burial. It takes some preparation. Usually I do it with several other women. Four, if possible. But everyone is busy, except for one woman. And so I was wondering if you would, that is, you wouldn't really have to do much, but just be there to give us a hand. In case we need you. Just in case."

Marne stared at Chaya. "Would I have to look at the body?"

Chaya took a deep breath. "Well, maybe. Probably. But she would be covered with a sheet. Most of the time, that is. It isn't gruesome. It's, well, it's a *mitzvah.*"

Marne nodded. At least she had learned that word. It had several meanings, all of them alluding to kindness, a good deed in God's eyes. And she had wondered, *Does God have eyes, anyhow?* Now she shuddered. Her fingers felt incredibly cold.

"I don't know," Marne began. "I've never seen a dead

person." She thought of Kim, telling her, and how Kim would say, "Yuck! You *didn't*! How gross!"

"I'd be there all the time," Chaya said. "Every minute. Maybe you'd just be there handing me things that I need. You wouldn't have to touch the . . . the dead woman. Look, I can understand if you feel reluctant."

"Creepy," Marne said.

"Creepy," Chaya acknowledged. "If you don't want to do it . . ."

"What would happen then?"

"Kalima and I will do our best. The thing is . . ."

"I'll come," Marne said, astonished at her own words. *Cool. Who would imagine such a thing? I'll tell people back home, "You'll never guess what I did this summer— yeah, stone-dead."* The most amazing thing Kim ever did was to go parasailing.

"Thank you, oh, thank you!" Chaya exclaimed, rushing out. "I'll explain everything on the way. We have to go now. Get the sandwiches, would you?"

In the kitchen Chaya rummaged through a drawer, grabbed her keys, stuffing them into her handbag, a large, lumpy, flowered satchel. "Yossi," she ordered, "bring me some towels from upstairs. Nissim, find Mama's handbook, the blue one. I think it's on my bureau. Jonathan,

119

go, go, check the carton. Hurry! Put everything into the back of the van, including the boards. Four boards. And check for rubber gloves and smocks."

"All right, all right," Jonathan muttered, shuffling out. He walked with an odd swagger, like a boy pretending to be a man.

"I wanna come!" yelled Yossi.

"Not this time," said Chaya, giving him a quick hug. "Mama needs you to stay here. You can watch the phone. Will you answer the telephone if it rings?"

"Yes! I'll say, 'Hello, this is the rabbi's house! Yossi speaking, can I help you?' "

"Excellent!" Chaya exclaimed, giving him another hug. "A real grown-up *person!*"

Bennie was on the floor again, his trousers wrapped around his legs. He lifted his arms imploringly, calling, "Up! Up!" Marne pulled him up, fixing his trousers. To her astonishment, he planted a wet kiss on her cheek.

"Let's go!" Chaya called, jiggling her keys. "Let's go!"

"What are the sandwiches for?" Marne asked as she and Chaya went to the van. All the children stood at the window to watch them leave.

"Us."

"How long will we be gone?"

"In these situations," Chaya said breathlessly, "you never know."

Kalima was a thin Hawaiian woman wearing a bright pink muumuu with white flowers. She smiled continually, called Marne "hon," and sat with her hands clutching the front seat, bracing herself as the car sped along the highway. As she drove, Chaya explained, speaking rapidly, rattling out the words. "Basically, we're just washing the person and dressing her in special white clothes. We have to pick out the casket. A plain pine box, hopefully. Nothing fancy. I hope they have a plain box. We treat the person with respect. As if she were alive. Only even better, because her soul . . ."

Chaya paused, checked the road sign. Kalima took up the explanation. "Actually, hon, the person is still there. The soul. Watching. Hovering. I learned all this in my conversion course."

"It's a great *mitzvah,*" added Chaya.

"Because it's a kindness that can't be repaid," said Kalima.

A sense of dread filled Marne. What if she got sick to

her stomach? What if she barfed? What if, oh, God—what if she started to giggle? Sometimes she couldn't help it. It just came over her, that fit of laughter, leaving her heaving and helpless. It was, her mother said, nervousness. She must learn to control it. Sure.

"Will I have to look at—the face?" she asked hesitantly.

Kalima leaned forward and patted Marne's hand. "Now, hon, it's really not so bad. The face will be covered."

"Most of the time," said Chaya. She executed a sharp left turn.

"And the body, too," added Kalima. "For modesty."

Marne nodded and stared straight ahead at the buildings, the palm trees, the traffic with its harsh sounds and the occasional motorbike blasting by with its blaze of smoke. It was incredibly hot, and Marne wore her capri pants and a long-sleeved shirt. As they left, Chaya had stared at her, opened her mouth, and closed it again with a determined look. "Let's go! You'll wear a gown when we . . . never mind."

Now she turned into a driveway beside a clapboard building with a sign out front: MORTUARY.

Two men came out to meet them. One wore a light gray summer suit and a white shirt with a navy blue tie.

"I'm James Bradshaw, the director. We are so sorry for your loss."

Marne felt it coming. Laughter. She took a deep breath, swallowed hard.

The other man, younger and dressed in a green golf shirt, looked harried and tense. His glance swept from one to the other, staying the longest on Marne. "Are you—the burial society?"

"Yes, indeed," said Chaya. "We came as soon as we could. You must be her cousin."

"Mark Phebes," he said with a nod. "Actually, she is—was—a second cousin. I hardly knew her. But she was on a tour of Hawaii, and she . . ." He looked flustered. "She was only sick for three days. Heart attack. In the hospital she told me she wanted . . ." He moistened his lips. "A Jewish burial. The real thing."

"Well, you came to the right place," Chaya said. Kalima nodded and smiled. "We need help with our supplies," Chaya said. "I have a couple of cartons in the back of the van."

The young man swayed nervously from one foot to the other. "I have a plane reservation at seven this evening. She'll be buried in Texas."

Chaya glanced at her watch. "Then we'd better get

started," she said briskly. She approached the director. "What is her name?"

Mark Phebes looked up, startled. "Her name was—is—Daisy."

"And her mother's name?" Chaya persisted.

"I don't know. I think—Bertha."

Chaya nodded and smiled slightly. "Daisy *bas* Bertha. Now, we'll need a plain wooden casket, pine, preferably. Do you have one?"

"Yes, indeed!" James Bradshaw stood at attention. "One. Just one. Most people, you see, prefer something a bit more ornamental for a final resting—"

"A plain pine box," Chaya emphasized, looking at Mark Phebes. "That's important."

Phebes jiggled the coins in his pocket. "I'll take care of it," he said. "Whatever you say. I had no idea—I mean, I didn't know she had a heart condition. How could I have known?"

"I'm sure she relied on you," said Chaya. "At the end. You were a comfort."

Mark Phebes wiped the back of his neck with his hand. "I hope so," he said. "I hardly knew her."

"It doesn't matter. Even if she was a stranger to you, you're doing a wonderful thing. Believe me," Chaya said.

124

Lightly she took Marne by the arm, leading her inside to the lobby.

The first thing that hit Marne was a blast of air-conditioning. Then she noticed the decor, almost like a hotel lobby, white wicker couches and chairs, a dark maroon carpet with a muted pattern of leaves, matching the tall plants that clung to the corners of the room. On the desk were a guest book and a sign, SERVICE WITH DIGNITY, and a stack of brochures listing funeral features and their prices. It all felt unreal, like Halloween, when people dress up as ghosts or zombies. She had never been inside a funeral home before.

Marne followed Chaya and Kalima down the somber hallway into a large white-tiled room that looked like a hospital surgery, with several large basins, a gurney, and, in the middle, a metal table on which lay a form covered with a sheet.

"She's all yours, ladies," said the director, holding the door open.

Chaya led the way. Then came Kalima, and, last, Marne stepped inside just as Chaya drew back the sheet. "Daisy," she murmured, as if meeting a new acquaintance, but softly, almost like a song. Then she drew back. "Oh, my," Chaya breathed. "Oh, *my*."

Marne took a step closer. Gingerly she peered at the

person, staring, holding her breath against the fits and gasps that surely were coming.

On the table lay a woman, a mass of sagging flesh that filled the table entirely and spilled out over the edges.

"Baruch Hashem!" exclaimed Kalima. "Praise God! She must weigh at least two hundred and fifty pounds!"

Marne bit her lips together, but she was unable to stop the sound that erupted from her mouth, which Chaya and Kalima interpreted as a cry of pity.

"Oh, Marne, it's all right!" cried Chaya. "She's at peace now."

"There, there, hon," murmured Kalima, her hand on Marne's shoulder. "It's a good thing you came. We'll definitely need you to help wash and dress her." Kalima handed her a green smock and rubber gloves, murmuring, "Put these on, hon."

No way, Marne thought. *Impossible. We are three women, small and slender. Not equipped for this—this job. Yes, think of it as a job. No, think of it as a* mitzvah. She was astonished that the strange word sprang so easily into her mind.

chapter NINE

No-no-no-no, I can't do this, Marne pleaded inwardly. She scanned the room, seeking escape. Her chest felt tight; she was going to be sick. But Chaya's voice, calm and clear, interrupted Marne's panic. She felt herself returning to the present and the task.

"Kalima, please get the buckets," Chaya said softly. "Fill all three of them at the basin."

Kalima glided to the basin and filled a square white plastic bucket with water. From the carton she took a gleaming steel pot, filled it, and proceeded to wash her hands, pouring water three times over her right hand, then three times over the left.

"Now you do it, hon," she told Marne, smiling warmly.

Marne poured the water over her hands, under Kalima's watchful eye, hearing her murmur, "That's right, hon. That's just fine."

Kalima handed her one of Chaya's towels to dry her hands, then a pair of thin rubber gloves and a pale green surgical mask. "Put these on, hon. And this smock. There you go."

Chaya, washed and gloved, stood at the head of the dead woman and gently covered her face with a thin white cloth.

Marne gazed at Chaya and Kalima, their silent movements and flowing gait, clad in pale green smocks like surgeons. She wanted to speak. She held her breath, feeling an absurd laughter bubbling within. It was so—weird that she, Marne, was standing over this corpse—no, they said it is a *person,* a mound of nearly formless flesh hanging over the edges of the gurney, white as a beached dolphin. She was so fat that the separate parts of her body seemed to melt together. Marne held her breath, closed her eyes, tried to focus on the antiseptic smell of the room, the gown, the mask, and the gloves. She opened her eyes, and at once her senses felt confused, hearing and seeing coalesced in a strange, out-of-body sensation.

Chaya was murmuring, "Daisy, daughter of Bertha, we of *Chevra Kadisha* ask your permission to perform a *taharah* on you. We ask your forgiveness for any disruption we cause you and for any error we might make."

Chaya nodded to Kalima. Kalima lifted one of the

woman's pudgy hands. "Two rings," Kalima said. She was perspiring; patches of dampness showed under her arms and around her neck. "I can't get them off."

"Use a little soap," Chaya said.

Marne heard the *slide-tick, slide-tick* of the large wall clock. At last Kalima exhaled sharply. "There. I've got them. And the watch." She slipped the jewelry into a small plastic bag.

"For the relatives, hon," she murmured to Marne. She proceeded to saturate a bit of cotton with polish remover. "Nail polish," she breathed, gently rubbing the woman's nails. Marne watched, entranced, as the cotton became stained with red.

"Why—" she began.

"Shh," said Chaya, frowning. "Don't talk. Unless it's necessary." She leaned over the woman, gently closed the eyelids.

"We cut the fingernails," Kalima whispered. "Toenails, too." She took a nail clipper from Chaya's carton and began.

Marne stared at the toes, large and deformed. And she remembered, with a sickening jolt in her chest, how when baby Jody first came home from the hospital, Mom unwrapped the blanket and showed Marne. "Look at those adorable little toes!" Tiny and pink, perfectly formed, the toes had taken Marne's breath away, and in that instant she had been filled with wonder.

Marne glanced up, gasping. A thin ribbon of blood ran down from the corner of the woman's mouth. "Look—she's bleeding!"

Instantly, Chaya seized a small wooden block and laid it under the head, reaching out for the gauze that Kalima held in readiness. "Don't worry," Chaya whispered, "it's quite normal. There." As if she was suddenly aware of Marne's presence, she said, "Please put fresh water into the buckets, Marne. Keep it coming."

Marne went to the sink and watched the water flow into the bucket. She couldn't seem to collect her thoughts. Impressions kept changing, flashing into her mind, swiftly flying away. Dead. Body. Blob. Water. Cold. The smell. Features, unyielding, like hardening clay. And the procedure, the movements so ordinary but odd, as if they were aliens trespassing on some sacred place. What right had she to be here? But Chaya had asked her, no, begged her, implying some terrible need—what? To wash this person before they laid her into the dirt? What sense did that make?

130

Words from other times, seeping through the walls, hummed back at her: *"They have these crazy rituals, keep themselves busy, thousands of details . . ."*

The person—what was her name? A strange, cartoony name, a flower—Daisy. Yes, Daisy. Someone named her for a flower with many petals—she loves me, she loves me not. Had anyone really loved Daisy? Had she loved herself? She probably had a job in some office and came home at night and ordered pizza or Chinese takeout. From the looks of her, she loved fried food. Or maybe she was on a perpetual diet and drank stuff to make her thin, only it didn't work. Like anyone else, Daisy combed her hair and took in the mail, had a job, polished her nails. Marne glanced at the nails, set into the fleshy fingers. They were large and newly shaped, perfectly squared. So, she was proud of her nails. Maybe they were her best feature. Maybe she fantasized about becoming a hand model, seeing photographs of her hands in a magazine. She had spent a good sum of money on that manicure, Marne thought. She had gone into the beauty shop, selected that color, maybe to match a shirt or a dress. Now the nails looked slightly yellowed and worn, as if they had been assaulted, denuded.

Jody always wanted her toenails painted—those tiny little nails. Mom used to paint them when she did her own; it was a ritual.

"These people have a thousand silly rituals . . ."

It seemed mean to have removed the polish so carefully selected, with never a notion that this would be her last manicure. Last day. If Daisy had known, what might she have done differently? Eaten more? Pies and ice cream and French fries, saying, "The hell with it! Eat, drink, and be merry, for tomorrow . . ."

Of course, she wasn't born fat. Most babies fall into narrow parameters, within two pounds or so. Marne herself was six pounds, two ounces. Jody weighed four ounces more. This woman—what might she have weighed at birth? Certainly not fifty pounds, no way! The thought almost made Marne burst out in one of her giggles. *Calm down, think rationally. Try to imagine how many doughnuts and French fries and cream pies it had taken to pump up that body like a huge balloon. Think of it as a talent. One had to be relentless in the pursuit of fat.*

Bitch. Marne's throat felt constricted. How horrible she was, judging this woman who had come to Hawaii for a vacation, with high hopes and desires. Looking for adventure, she was, looking for romance. Why not? Everyone longs for romance, even old people, ugly people, fat people. Her mom said so. It was the key to effective marketing. Just look around. Old men and women would sit on the benches facing the sea, glancing at each other like teenagers. Soon they were talking about the weather, then sharing a croissant while they shared stories, and later he might touch her hand and she would slap at his arm in a playful gesture, laughing.

So this person, this woman, Daisy, collected her savings and set out for Hawaii, looking for romance. She had this distant cousin in Hawaii, someone to call, so she told the others in her tour group, "Oh, sorry, my dears, I can't join the rest of you for dinner, because I have this prior date with a distant cousin." Distant, implying possibilities, someone waiting in the wings. Someone. Death.

Marne gasped, stunned by the drama, the reality: Death had come sneaking up on poor Daisy. Now Marne opened her eyes fully and looked at the woman's face. The features were slack, but surprisingly fine. The nose was slender and well formed, the lips pointed, the bottom lip fleshy. Her cheekbones were wide set, like the broad faces of Eskimo women that Marne had seen pictured in *National Geographic*. This fat woman had gone to Hawaii for romance and adventure and found Death instead, and now she lay helpless while her body was being bathed by strangers.

"It is a *mitzvah*," Kalima whispered suddenly, as if she could read Marne's thoughts. "A great *mitzvah*, because the person can give nothing in return. It is a pure kindness."

Marne nodded. "There's polish on her toenails," she whispered. The polish was silver. How had Kalima missed it? Was that her mission here, to clean dead toenails?

"Do you want to remove it, Marne?"

Marne nodded and whispered, "Yes. I will," and she took the cotton soaked with remover and bent over Daisy, taking care not to look too closely, like that first day in middle school when everybody had to strip and take a shower and all the girls tried to avoid looking at each other, being cool.

Marne took the large, solid foot in her hand and began wiping gently, but resolutely, first the big toe, then each of the others, her entire being focused on this task as if the fate of the world depended upon it.

What would her mom say? "You *didn't*. You *wouldn't*!" she'd shriek. "What possessed you? I never heard of such a thing."

What would Kim say? "Awesome." And she would laugh hysterically.

Her dad would nod and say, "Nothing surprises me anymore," but he wore that perpetual look of surprise.

When she was done, Marne walked over to the waste can and put the stained cotton into it, hearing the squeaking of her tennis shoes as they hit the linoleum. She watched as Chaya wrung out a cloth from the bucket of water and gently wiped the woman's face, as one might wipe a baby. Firmly, with a humming sound under her breath, Chaya lifted one arm and washed, intent on her task, then the chest, lifting the bulbous breast, replacing it slowly. Slowly she moved across the belly, down to the hip, the thigh, all in rhythm, her eyes slightly glazed, as if she were really on a different plane and it was only her body performing these acts, quite apart from her being. Marne realized that Chaya was praying.

"You must help me turn her." The words caught Marne by surprise, as if she had been watching a silent film and suddenly sound intruded. "Marne, come here to her shoulder. Kalima, there. On three. We can do it. Together. One, two . . ."

Marne felt the perspiration spreading under her arms,

down her sides, on her neck and forehead. She began to murmur to herself, singing in her mind the four notes that repeated and repeated, four notes from somewhere else, somewhere she had never been before. *La-la-da-dee* . . . the notes were like a raft, a life jacket, keeping her afloat.

Slowly the body shifted, slipped back, resisting, while equally intent the three of them pushed and pushed, Marne holding her breath, minding the notes, *la-la-da-dee*. Marne held her stance, tightened her grip. Kalima murmured something under her breath. Chaya signaled with her eyes: "Hold it. Here." She took the cloth and wiped, wiped, wiped. . . .

And Marne felt breathless and wet, as if it were she being bathed, purified. The sleeves of her smock were drenched. Her feet felt damp. Maybe she was being baptized. How ridiculous! Now the laughter rose dangerously to her chest, her throat, threatening to erupt, and while Marne knew it was only the release of stress and anxiety, still she was unable to stop it. She grunted. She groaned, made herself cough, and it came out in a snort, three sharp blasts.

". . . out . . . for a moment . . . ," Marne gasped.

Kalima, sweet, understanding Kalima, nodded toward the door, toward fresh air and freedom and the terrible, wonderful relief of letting the giggles and the agony explode.

Marne stood there in the dark hall, holding her sides as if she must literally keep herself from falling apart. She pulled off the rubber gloves. Her own hands on her own flesh were somehow reassuring. She closed her eyes, opened them again, and felt the sweet relief of just being, just breathing. Never before had she been thankful for breath.

When after several minutes she returned, it was like a traveler coming home. This time it took only a moment and she was part of a group, moving, thinking, *being* together as if they were making music.

"Now the shower," Chaya whispered. Kalima nodded, and Marne understood the reason for the drains in the floor and the blocks of wood that Chaya had placed under the shoulders and hips. They would pour water over the entire body and let it drip down, a final cleansing.

The flow of the water from the faucet into the bucket, the feel of water on her hands had a soothing effect, an almost hypnotic effect, as Marne moved from the sink to the gleaming steel table with Daisy upon it. She listened to the sounds of water splashing, cascading, while the three of them stood by, each pouring slowly from a bucket, their movements somehow synchronized as in a dance, three people in motion, three living women ministering to another, who lay motionless but seemed somehow aware, needing this final touch from the physical plane as she moved to a place that was more tender, more peaceful than any she had known before.

"Now the clothes." All in white they dressed her, white bonnet and loose white trousers, white jacket. As the two women grunted and strained, Marne found herself working with them, lifting first one leg, then the other, all revulsion and anxiety gone. Her hands did not tremble; she felt an utter calm as she helped press the thick arms into sleeves, then watched Chaya and Kalima tie the strings on the sleeves and front of the jacket. Chaya lit a small candle and placed it at Daisy's feet, once again expressing their apologies for any errors or omissions.

They stood silent for a long moment, reluctant to leave. And Marne felt a strange connectedness with everyone here, especially with the woman who lay in deep repose, serene as an angel.

"We leave now," Kalima whispered, walking backward. She took Marne's hand, and Marne felt the warm flesh with a strange sense of joy. Kalima's hand vibrated with life.

"May we meet again," Chaya intoned, "at a joyous occasion."

"Amen!" exploded Kalima with such energy that Marne allowed her laughter to cascade freely. And to her amazement, Chaya was laughing softly, too.

chapter TEN

She woke up screaming. It took a moment to realize that the screams had come from her own mouth and that her body was slick with sweat. Becca's terrified face loomed before her and Chaya rushed in, looking frantic.

"What is it? What is it? Are you hurt?"

"Dreams," Marne gasped. Her throat felt constricted.

"What was the dream?"

She shook her head. She could not say the words. She'd been driving the car on the wrong side of the road, up a hill, sliding into ruts and huge rocks and rubble. Beneath the rubble she saw bodies, only partly buried.

Chaya sat down on the bed. She laid her hand on Marne's forehead. "You're so hot! Come. Let's sit out in the yard for a few minutes. We'll drink some juice. There's a lovely breeze."

Marne shook her head. "I—no. I don't want to go outside."

"What do you want to do?"

"Nothing. Just sleep."

Chaya glanced around the room, as if to find help. "All right," she said at last. "If you need anything . . ."

"I'm fine now, Aunt Chaya. Really. Thanks."

"I'll leave the light on," Chaya said. She wore a long white cotton nightgown, and her hair, the same auburn as Marne's mom's, stood up around her head.

"Your hair," Marne said thickly. "What happened to your hair?"

Chaya gave a slight chuckle. "It's on my bureau."

And Marne realized with a jolt that Chaya's long, sleek copper-colored hair was a wig. It angered her, somehow. Nothing was as it seemed, or as it was supposed to be. Summer in Hawaii was supposed to be filled with long, lazy days, swimming in the ocean, surfing, getting tan, hanging out with other kids on the beach. Instead, there were the endless chores, drives to the store, fixing crafts for the grimy little campers, playing her guitar for a bunch of staring five- and six-year-olds who couldn't keep a tune in a bucket. And to top it off, she felt like a weirdo— and why? Because she wore shorts and tank tops and a bathing suit that didn't look like something out of the Victorian Age. She was the normal one. They were the weird ones, with rules for everything. All she wanted was some fun, like everyone else who came to the islands. She'd been tricked. They had her in a box. Tomorrow she'd call her father, insist that he let her come home.

Becca turned to her, propped up on her elbow.

"Want to talk?"

"No. Thanks. Go to sleep."

Rebuffed, Becca turned away, her hunched-up body, wrapped in the summer blanket, implying reproach.

I don't care, Marne thought. *I didn't ask for this.* Her mother had warned her: *"Don't think you're going to get a free ride. Carole will expect you to help. She'll expect you to fall in line with the house rules. She can be very controlling."*

So, what else is new? Marne had wanted to retort, but she had held her tongue. Once she got going, her mom was really launched.

"Carole was always an extremist, one way or another. In high school she hung out with a bunch of hippies. Wore nothing but sandals and those long, limp skirts. They played guitars and recorders and looked like hell. Most of 'em flunked out of school. I don't know how Carole managed to graduate. She kept a bong in her underwear drawer. I always knew it was there."

"Did you tell your parents?" Marne had asked.

Her mother had shrugged. "No. Anyhow, my mother wouldn't have believed me. She was always great with denial. If I told her Carole was into pot, she'd just call me an idiot and go out shopping."

"What about Grandpa?"

Her mother had frowned, tossing her hair. "What about Grandpa?" She lit a long cigarette, took a deep drag, and let the smoke stream out thickly. She only smoked three a day, she said, on the way to quitting. Sure. When she was eight, Marne had hidden her mom's cigarettes in the garage, under the water heater. Later it was evident that rats had gotten into the tobacco; bits of it were strewn on the floor. And Marne had asked her father whether rats could get lung cancer, and he had laughed uproariously. "Want to hear something cute?" He repeated the story to friends, over and over, and they always laughed. Of course, her mother bought new packs of cigarettes, even a whole carton, which she kept high on the kitchen shelf, behind the old toaster oven.

Becca's breathing evened out. Good. Marne didn't want to talk. She needed, needed . . . something. Like a smoker needs a cigarette. Like an addict needs the drug of choice.

Marne leaned out of her bed and reached for the book.

She sat back against the pillows, her knees drawn up, and she went through it page by page, mouthing the words, absorbing the pictures that she had already memorized but desperately needed to see again. As she sat there, half entranced, Marne heard them through the walls, Chaya and Yitz, their voices rising, as the voices of her own parents often did.

"You—*what*? A girl like that, vulnerable? A fifteen-year-old girl?"

". . . had to, Yitz. There was nobody. . . ."

"I can't believe you'd be so insensitive. . . ."

"I asked her! She said she would."

"How could she refuse? You gave her no choice."

"She agreed. I didn't force her!"

"But we're keeping her for the summer. She'd feel indebted, don't you see?"

"Yitz, she didn't mind. It was a learning experience."

"I can't believe . . . How can you inflict this on your own niece? She's a child!"

"She's a *woman*. Under Jewish law, a woman!"

"Good heavens, Chaya! The first law is toward compassion!"

Marne bit her lip, hard. Tomorrow she'd call her father and make him let her come home. Maybe he could change his work schedule. Or she'd go to the hospital with him at night—sure, why not? Maybe even do some volunteer work or get a job fetching bedpans. Why not? After getting a dead person ready for burial, bedpans would be easy.

"But she had to be properly buried, Yitz. Why can't you see that?"

"It wasn't Marne's job! It wasn't her responsibility!"

"My God, Yitz, I try to do everything. . . ."

"Maybe that's the problem. Just do your share. And don't use God's name in vain. . . ."

"Stop lecturing me, Yitz! My God!"

Marne put the book under the bed. She pulled the sheet up over her shoulders and snapped out the light. In sixth grade there was a boy, Stuart, kind of short and fat, and when he was mad he'd say, "Oh my heck!" Everyone laughed and mimicked him. He'd stand there looking like a little deacon and scold about using God's name in vain. The kids laughed at him and yelled out, "Oh my heck!" jumping up and down. After spring vacation Stuart never came back, and Marne had felt bad and guilty, because she'd been in on it, too.

What's the big deal? Everyone said *God* when they were surprised or upset. It was a regular exclamation.

145

They weren't really thinking about *God,* though. That was the thing; Yitz and Chaya and even the kids seemed to be thinking about God all the time, as if He was living in the house somewhere, invisible, but steadily watching to see what they wore, what they ate, and listening constantly for appreciation. Why did God need to be praised all the time? And why would God care if you used His name in vain?

When she was little, Marne had a Catholic babysitter who taught her to pray before she went to sleep: "Now I lay me down . . ." Then Marne asked God for things, like a real monkey or for the rain to stop so they could play on the beach. She never got the monkey. The rain had lasted for four days in a row. It was all in vain. Like the prayers that were said in their living room the Friday night after Jody vanished, a bunch of strangers crowding into the room, acting as if they had a right to be there, some of the men wearing little black caps on the back of their heads. They even gave her dad a little cap to wear, as if it mattered.

"Of course," her mom had said. "No harm in trying." Her hair looked ragged. She wore the same skirt and stained blouse she'd been wearing for the past three days. Marne was wearing shorts and a red-and-white-checked shirt, the only freshly laundered clothes in her drawer, the rest of her things still stuffed into her suitcases from camp.

Afterward, when the people were all gone, the house felt isolated and eerily silent. No words remained, for none sufficed. No condolence or hope or prayer made any difference; they all ended in vain. In silence. So Marne had gone into her room and taken the book from the shelf and read it, seeking clues. Somewhere there had to be a clue, because little girls don't just vanish, do they?

Detectives had questioned her parents, both together, then separately. And Marne knew they were looking for clues. They had questioned Marne. "Does your father get angry with you? Does he ever spank you? What does he do when you are naughty? You can tell us. We'll take care of you. Did he ever . . . ? Did he ever . . . ? Did your mother ever . . . ?"

"No. He never. No, my mom never . . ." And she knew what kind of clues they were looking for, acting so friendly and kind, squinting and smiling with concern, calling her "dear" and "sweetheart," until at last she sprang up, enraged, yelling, "I'm not your sweetheart!"

It had taken hours for the anger to subside, hours and a small pill that Mom made her take with orange juice. Then came the sleep that pulled her under, as if she were buried and could not extricate herself, no matter how hard she tried. When finally she awakened, it was a new world, a world where nobody dared to move too quickly or think too deeply or say anything that might make the goblins come again. Because they had stolen Jody, and nobody knew what they were planning to do with her, and if they remained very quiet, it might just turn out all right, and Jody would be there in the morning, asleep in her own bed.

Marne lay on her back, listening to Becca's breathing. Still the fight rumbled through the walls. Chaya was crying.

"I never force anybody to do anything. . . ."

"But you do. You may not know it, but you do. You're like an engine, you just go full steam ahead. . . ."

"I thought that's what you like about me."

"I do, Chaya, but I'm an adult. I can resist. I can balance. . . ."

Becca's voice intruded. "I hate it when they fight. They say they don't. They just call it a 'discussion.'"

"My parents do the same thing. They fight and deny it."

"Was it awful? The *taharah*?"

"Yes," she said. "And no. After a little while I got used to the idea. I guess you can get used to anything."

"How could you stand it? The idea creeps me out."

148

"Me too," Marne admitted.

"Why did you do it, then?"

"Curiosity."

"To see a dead person?"

"To see if I could handle it."

Becca sighed. "I wish I were brave."

Marne chuckled. "I think you're pretty brave to handle all those wild kids in day camp."

Now Becca quickly pulled herself up on one elbow, blurting out, "Do you still look for Jody? I mean, every day?"

Marne felt her heart lurch. "Yes. I suppose I do."

"If you found her . . ."

Anguish flooded over Marne, like a tidal wave obliterating the possibility of speech. So sudden was the question, so deep and swift the pain. She glanced up and saw the remorse in Becca's eyes. "I'm sorry! I'm so sorry!"

Marne took a long breath. "It's okay, Becca. It's like— I know you know, and we struggle around it, trying not to talk about it. About her. Jody."

"I know," Becca whispered, the sheet drawn up to her lips, so that her eyes looked out, large and almost golden. "I guess if you found her, if she came back . . ."

"I think about it all the time," Marne said, and it was

149

as if a heavy cloak were slipping from her shoulders as the words slid from her lips. "And I wonder how it would feel. Would she even know us? Would we recognize her? Five years is a long time. She was only six. It's nearly double her life. What did they tell her? What happened to her? Did she forget us? I hear things on TV, you know, stories about lost children. One girl turned up after twelve years! Her parents had never stopped looking, never lost hope. The dad found her somehow, living in Georgia with this old couple. Their daughter had died of some awful illness, so they just picked up this little girl and kept her. They'd told the girl her parents were dead and they had come to take her home and take care of her. She was thirteen when the dad found her. I don't know how. DNA, I guess. Anyhow, it was so weird. They showed it on TV, how the dad came to get her, and the girl was completely shaken and confused. She didn't want to leave that old couple. She couldn't remember her dad and mother."

"What happened? Did she go back with her father?" Becca was chewing the ends of her hair; the swatch of coppery hair dissected her cheek, almost like a scar.

"I don't know. My mom came home then, and I turned it off. I don't want her to see things like that, and she . . ." Marne felt the shiver start along her back, the trembling that would, in a moment, gather into her fingers. And she saw, as if it were played before her eyes, the many times each of them had changed the subject, turned off the TV, walked out of a movie, or walked out of the house to avoid the next word, the next thought, the next possible truth.

"We try," Marne said softly, her voice trembling, "we try to pretend that we don't think about it."

Becca, wide-eyed, nodded. She pushed her hair back from her face, and she suddenly looked older than twelve. "I got my period today," she announced. "First time. Nobody knows, except my mom."

Marne felt the laughter rising in her chest, incongruous, silly, wonderful laughter. "Congratulations," she said. "Now you don't have to wonder when—or where—it will start." She saw, of course, that Becca's statement was meant as a gift, a secret.

"It feels strange. Like something is sort of tipping over inside of me."

"I know."

"Don't tell Jonathan."

"Of course not. I—I remember I didn't want my dad to know."

"Did he ever find out yet?"

Marne laughed. "I'm sure he figured it out."

They were silent for a long moment. Then Marne said, "If Jody were here, if we did find her, she'd be nearly your age. She'd look so different. Maybe I wouldn't even recognize her. I suppose I could pass her at the mall and never know. . . ."

"Want to go to the mall with me next week?"

"Will your mom let us go?"

"Yes. I already asked her. My grandma sent me fifty dollars for my birthday."

"Your grandma is my grandma."

"I know. Isn't that neat?" Becca giggled. "I've got forty-five dollars to spend. I want to get some new tops. You can help me pick them out. You have a great sense of color," she said soberly.

"You said fifty dollars."

"Five goes to *tzedakah*."

"Charity?"

"Ten percent. I figure I can probably get two tops and something else, maybe an accessory."

"Accessories are nice," Marne said, settling down under the sheet.

"You can turn off the light now," Becca said. "I don't mind the dark."

"Me neither," said Marne.

She listened to the breeze from outside, the branches of the heliotrope tree gently rubbing together, and she pictured the gnarled roots protruding out of the ground, seeking nourishment from the most unlikely source, from salt water.

She heard faint, whispered words and she knew Becca was saying her prayers. Maybe Becca was praying for her, too. She remembered something Yitz had said last *Shabbos* to the people gathered in the living room, sitting on folding chairs and floor cushions.

"Just have a conversation with God once in a while. Talk to Him, like a friend. He wants to hear from you, to know what's going on."

Someone had asked, "But doesn't God know everything? Why do we have to tell Him?"

Yitz smiled in his quiet way. "The telling is for you," he said. "To make the connection."

The four notes that had kept her afloat at the mortuary formed into words: *Are You there, God?* She thought of the book by Judy Blume and added, *It's me, Marne Lewison, Jody's sister. . . . I need to ask You some important questions. . . .*

chapter ELEVEN

"Put it on the list," Esti squealed, hopping up and down, pulling on Marne's arm. "Purple ribbons. And some glitter."

"I don't need a list, Esti," Marne said, biting her lip. It was exasperating. Going to the mall with Becca turned out to be major. First Chaya had to make a list of everything they were supposed to look for. Chaya and her lists! Post-it lists were stuck onto the telephone, the cupboards, and the walls, everything from grocery lists to people who needed phone calls because they were sick or lonely or coming for *Shabbos*.

"Does your mom want you to have glitter?"

"Why not?" said Chaya, rushing in with the baby on her hip. "Yossi, come on, honey. You and Bennie are going for your checkup. Yossi, bring Mama's diaper bag, that's a good boy. Jonathan, help Nissim with his model while we're gone. Twins, you have a playdate with Leslie. Her mom is coming for you. Get your shoes on, Esti! Come on, let's get this show on the road!"

At last they were settled in the car, and Marne shoved the list into her shoulder bag, a large, multicolored patchwork. Becca, sitting beside her, jiggled with anticipation, smoothing back her hair, lifting and replacing her headband constantly.

"Have you got your wallet?" Chaya asked as she left them off.

"Yes, Mom. I'll have Marne keep it in her bag."

"Fine. Now, we'll meet you back here in exactly two hours. This entrance. Remember it."

"Don't worry, Chaya," Marne said. "We'll be here."

"And don't forget Esti's ribbons, please. She's been driving me crazy."

"We'll get everything, I promise," Marne said, hoping they would find all the stuff on that list: a pacifier for the baby, a bathing suit for Elias, two beach towels to replace those that the campers had ruined, some pieces of lace, red thread or string, a large package of beads . . . The list was ridiculous, Marne thought, but it was worth it to get away for a couple of hours. And Becca was excited.

"Let's go for me first," Becca said. She ran to the

directory to locate her favorite boutique. "Here, it's on the third floor. Hurry!"

"Let's take the elevator," Marne said. "Since you're in a hurry."

"Okay."

The elevator skimmed down, the doors slid open, and a horde of people emerged. Someone called out, "Marne! What are you doing here?"

She whirled around, and immediately her heart hammered as Jeff hurried in beside her. His hair was curly and sun-streaked, rather longer than before, and he was wearing a pale yellow T-shirt that set off his tan, and cargo shorts with rows of small pockets down his legs. "I'll ride up with you," he offered, smiling broadly.

"I thought you just came down."

"Now I'm going up! How great to see you."

A song poured out from the speakers, matching Marne's joyful mood. It was as if she had been waiting for him, and now he stood right beside her. "Where have you been?" she said. "I never see you on the beach anymore." She hoped she didn't sound too whiny, as if she owned him or something.

"I tore my Achilles tendon," Jeff said, moving closer as several people entered the elevator.

The elevator's rise took Marne's breath away. Or maybe it was Jeff standing so close that she could feel a warmth from his arm brushing hers.

"Oh, that's too bad. I guess that means no surfing."

"No surfing, no jogging, no tennis. It's a bummer."

They had arrived on the third floor, joining the throng of shoppers in the corridor.

"Come on," Becca said, looking past Jeff, her face placid, as if he were invisible.

"Jeff, this is my cousin Becca," Marne quickly said.

"Hi, Becca," Jeff said with a nod and a smile. "How're you doing?"

"Okay," Becca mumbled. Her lips moved wordlessly, adding something else. Marne knew what it was. Becca and her family always added the words *baruch Hashem*— "praise God." She froze, conscious now of Becca's awkward denim skirt and thick socks, and the long-sleeved blouse. She looked quaint and old-fashioned and feverish from the sultry heat.

"Becca's shopping with her birthday money," Marne explained, feeling desperate. "Where's your boutique, Becca?"

"There, right there," Becca said, pointing. "Come on!"

"There's a juice bar down there across the way," Jeff

said, pointing. "I thought I'd sit down and maybe you can join me."

"We'd love to!" Marne exclaimed.

"See you in a few!" Jeff waved and walked on.

"Let's go get your clothes." Marne grasped Becca's arm. "Then we can have some juice."

"I don't think it's kosher," Becca said. "Besides, I want to go to the other store, too."

"Maybe you'll find what you want right here!" Marne cried. She picked up a blue top with a large silk-screened lily on the front. "Look, isn't this darling? This would look terrific with your skirt." She flipped over the tag. "It's only thirty-two dollars," she exclaimed. "Try it on, Becca."

"I don't like it," Becca said. "I hate flowers on clothes."

"Flowers are darling on clothes. Everyone's wearing them!"

"It's way too expensive," Becca said. "If I buy that, I won't be able to get anything else."

Marne spotted a white shirt with an embroidered collar. "How about this?"

"It's not for me," Becca insisted, shaking her head. She picked up a pale lilac sweater. "What about this?"

Marne felt torn, her heart racing. That color with

158

Becca's hair would be devastating. But if she bought it they could go, go and be with Jeff. Or—her mind felt rattled, confused. Would Becca have some other excuse? Oh, God, why did this have to happen? No doubt there was some stupid rule about sitting at a table with a boy or drinking smoothies—who knew? There were so many pitfalls, so many crazy restrictions.

"I think you should try on several things," Marne said, trying to calm down and moderate her voice, as if she had all the time in the world. "Try the lilac and also the white and maybe that other blue one. Think about your skirts and what would match. I'll tell you what—these dressing rooms are so tiny, I'd have to wait out here for you. I'll be right there at the juice place. You see the sign? That red-and-green sign? Okay? You don't need me to try things on, do you?"

"Well, I want you to help me choose," Becca said, chewing the end of her hair. "I want you to tell me what looks good."

"Of course I will!" Marne exclaimed, gathering up an armful of tops, pressing them into Becca's arms. "You pick the best two or three and then come and get me. Then we'll decide together. It'll only take you five or ten minutes, and then we'll have plenty of time to go to other stores." She gazed at Becca's eyes, wide and filled with concern. "I promise," she added. "This is what Kim and I always do. We don't like being in the same dressing room. It's not . . . not *tznius,*" she added. *Brilliant,* she congratulated herself.

"Okay. But don't leave the juice place."

"Of course not." Marne went to the door, careful not to look as if she was rushing, while her heart was racing. She made herself walk at an ordinary pace, just in case Jeff was watching. She could see him sitting at a window table, looking out.

He rose as Marne approached, and he hurried to grab a chair for her. "Hey! I'm glad you came. I ordered you a strawberry cooler. Is that okay? Or do you want something else? I mean, maybe you're allergic to strawberries."

Marne laughed. "I love strawberries." She felt elated. He was so sweet, so considerate. Maybe he'd been thinking about her, too. He seemed a little nervous, twirling his straw in the foamy drink.

"Thanks," she said, taking a sip of her drink. "It's perfect."

"So," he said, "you're still running in the mornings. And you missed me."

She bit back a grin. "I didn't say that. Not exactly. What have you been doing?"

She glanced at his foot and the bandage.

"My dad's been taking me to his golf club. He always wanted me to learn golf. I was so mad about that torn tendon. Now it seems like there's a good side to it."

"You like golf?"

He shrugged. "I like being with my dad. I like being out there at the club. And Dad says I'm getting pretty good at it."

"That's great," Marne said. She took a long sip from her drink. "This is delicious."

"I wanted to see you," Jeff said. He twirled the straw round and round in his glass. "I even went to the house a couple of times."

"Why didn't you knock?"

"I did. Once nobody was home. The second time I heard all this commotion. . . ."

"That's standard," Marne said. "My aunt's got seven kids."

"Seven!"

"And guests half the time. You should have come in. They love guests."

"Your aunt obviously didn't like me."

"Oh, she was just upset because I was late."

Jeff gave her a long look. "I don't think so. She was mad."

From the speakers came the insistent, loud beats of a rap song. Several boys stopped in the corridor to do an impromptu dance. The mall was noisy and chill. Marne longed for quiet, for relief. "Actually, they were very nice to let me stay for the summer. Chaya's just, well, she's intense. Keeps this tight schedule."

Jeff looked unconvinced. "Do you have to babysit?"

"Well, of course I help them out," Marne said. The conversation had become complicated, and Marne wished they could go outside where the breezes were soft and pleasant. Marne glanced at her watch. It had been ten minutes, no, twelve. Well, Becca was probably having fun trying on clothes, acting grown up.

Jeff leaned toward her, frowning. "Your cousin seems so shy. Does she ever talk?"

"Oh, yes. All the time. I told you," she said, feeling defensive, "they have guests all the time, and Becca helps and she's very sociable. Really."

"Okay." Jeff held out his hand, as if to seek a truce. Marne shook his hand. It felt cool and warm at the same time. She didn't want to let go, but after a long moment, she did.

They sat quietly for a time, finishing their drinks. Then Marne said, "They are religious."

Jeff nodded. "I know. Chabad. Everyone knows."

"So?" Suddenly Marne felt defensive again. "They don't bother anyone. They just try to . . ."

"Yeah. I know. They try to get people to come to their synagogue, and they convert them. My dad told me. He knows all that stuff. He's Jewish."

"Oh!" Possibilities sprang up, amazing possibilities. "Really!" she exclaimed.

"Well, we don't *do* anything Jewish. My dad says the important thing is to be a good person. To keep your word and not to cheat anyone."

"I agree," Marne said quickly. "Actually, we don't do anything either. It's just my aunt. She sort of went off the deep end, according to my mom. But, you know, it's interesting. I mean, people go on those exchange programs to see how other people live. . . ."

Jeff nodded. "My cousin went to Argentina for two weeks and lived with a family. Then those kids came to the U.S. So," he said with a grin, "you're here on a cultural exchange program."

She smiled. "I guess so. Like, you never really know how it is until you live with people." She glanced around, wondering whether she ought to say this, but it bugged her. Who else did she have to talk to? "Listen, Becca can't even go swimming with her own brother. Really! She keeps this water pitcher and bowl by her bed and first thing in the morning, even before she can talk, she has to wash her hands."

"Why? Do they get dirty in the night?" Jeff looked intrigued.

Marne shrugged. "I don't know. I think it's something about the soul leaving your body when you're asleep, and reentering . . . I don't know. Anyhow, she washes her fingers from this water pitcher. They call it *negel vasser.*"

"What?" Jeff started to laugh, then he clapped his hand over his mouth. "I'm sorry. I shouldn't talk. My mom was raised as a Baptist. So, what does that make me? She thinks it's all a crock."

"My folks aren't into it either," Marne said. She took a deep breath, looked around at all the people here, everyone looking happy, free. "It's sort of a control issue."

"I know. My dad says they're all control freaks. They want everyone to believe what they do."

"Not only believe," Marne said. "They want you to *do* stuff."

Jeff nodded. "My mom quit the church when she was only fourteen." He frowned. "It took guts, but she left one Sunday and never stepped inside of a church again."

"How come?" Marne leaned toward him. Jeff was different now, serious, vulnerable. She wanted to take his hand, but she only looked into his eyes.

"Sin and wickedness, that's all those preachers talked about. Mom just got up one day and ran out and told her folks she wasn't wicked, she wasn't a sinner, and she wasn't going to go back there ever again."

"What happened?"

"She never went back. And neither did her parents. They even started having a little glass of wine once in a while."

"Wow!" Marne laughed. "We have wine all the time. Every Friday night and Saturday lunch. Even the little kids get a sip."

"Sounds great," Jeff said, settling back in his chair. "Maybe I should join you sometime."

Marne took a deep breath and braced herself. "Come Friday night," she said, "for dinner."

165

"Well, I don't know about that Friday-night thing," Jeff said slowly. "I guess you have a ceremony and everything. I've never been . . ."

"Think of it as a cultural exchange," Marne said.

"I guess it could be interesting. And you'll be there. You won't let them indoctrinate me."

"Oh, they always have new people. Don't worry, it's cool. Please come."

"Well, it sounds great. What time?"

Inadvertently Marne glanced at her watch and leaped up. "My gosh! We've been talking for so long. What could have happened to Becca? I have to go."

Jeff caught her arm. "Wait! Meet me in the morning. I'll clock you while you run. I can be your trainer! Not that you need one."

"Okay." Marne broke away, calling back, "Thanks. I'll see you tomorrow." Marne hurried along the wide corridor, dodging shoppers and children, feeling fearful and guilty. She'd spent over half an hour with Jeff, forgetting about Becca completely. Could she still be trying on clothes all by herself? What if she walked out and got lost? Could that really happen?

The boutique was filled with shoppers. Marne

searched through the entire store, even calling Becca's name outside the dressing rooms. There was no response. Marne stood at the counter behind several shoppers waiting to pay. Panic made her feel hot all over, made her heart pound. At last she got the clerk's attention. She was a thin girl with long straight blond hair, wearing low-rider jeans that showed the stud in her navel. Several rings vied for space at the side of her nose, and a silver stud lay on her tongue.

"Excuse me!" Marne said loudly, for the girl's gaze swept past her to a group of boys. "I'm looking for my cousin. She's twelve. She was wearing a denim skirt. Did you see her here?"

"I just came on ten minutes ago," the girl said, flinging back her hair. "Anyhow, I don't really notice people. Like, I'm just on the register, you know?"

Marne raised her voice. "But did you see her?"

"I told you, I didn't see nobody like that."

Marne whirled around, finally caught sight of a woman with a clerk's badge and demeanor, wearing a dark smock and sturdy shoes. She focused on the woman's face, on her message, fighting her rising panic. "Excuse me," she said, trying to maintain her composure, "I'm looking for my cousin. I was supposed to meet her here. She's twelve, with kind of copper-colored hair down to here and a long denim skirt. . . ."

"Oh, you're the one!"

"Is she here? I couldn't find her. What's wrong?"

"She's in the back. Being questioned by the police. You better come along with me." The woman turned, giving Marne a bitter look, and said with disgust, "You kids should be ashamed."

chapter TWELVE

Becca was sitting in a large swivel chair. It seemed to engulf her. The moment Marne opened the door, Becca shouted, "There she is!" She shot over to Marne, her eyes blazing. "Where were you? They wouldn't let me out. The buzzer went off. They called the police!"

A heavyset man dressed in a security uniform, white shirt, black trousers, and a picture ID on his pocket, said sternly, "This young lady was walking out with merchandise under her blouse. We've had a lot of shoplifting at this mall." He sat down on the desk, his stomach bulging out under his shirt.

Becca cried out, "I told them I was just going to get you! I forgot I had that blouse. . . ."

"Look, Officer," Marne began in a conciliatory tone. She knew better than to antagonize a cop. They had dealt with plenty of cops, and most of them wore that hard armor around themselves, defying anyone to expect sympathy.

"Becca's my cousin. She's not a thief. She just didn't realize . . ."

"She's doesn't have any ID. No money on her. Nothing." The man's eyes narrowed. "That's standard procedure with kids like this. No bags or backpacks to raise suspicion. They just walk out with the merchandise under their own clothes. We caught one kid—a boy—wearing five stolen shirts and three pairs of bathing trunks. Those baggy styles are perfect for shoplifters."

"I'm not a shoplifter!" Becca protested. "I've never stolen anything."

Marne reached into her bag. "Here's her wallet. I was keeping it for her. Look, Officer, Becca's only twelve years old, and she's been . . . I guess you could say sheltered. She never goes out alone."

Marne stole a look at Becca's face. It looked swollen, as if she'd been crying.

"Her parents are, like, they're missionaries. Jewish missionaries. Well, not exactly. Her father is a rabbi."

"A rabbi?" The officer squinted at Becca. "Your father is a rabbi?"

Becca gave a loud sniff. "Yes."

"All right. We'll just give him a call."

"Please don't call my father!" Becca cried.

"Would you rather come in to the station?" the guard demanded, holding up the receiver and squinting at Becca's ID. After a long moment he punched in the numbers, and Marne could hear the answering machine click on: "Shalom! This is Rabbi Kessler. Please leave a message and I'll return your call ASAP. Have a great day!"

"Rabbi . . . ," the guard began. Then he looked at the receiver and slammed it down. He stood opposite Becca, legs apart as if he were lecturing a squadron, and he pointed his finger accusingly. "I'm going to go easy on you this time. Next time you go anywhere, you keep your ID with you. And don't ever, *ever* walk out of a store with an item you haven't paid for."

Becca thrust out her chin. "I never meant to—"

"She won't, Officer," Marne said hastily. "We have to go. Come *on*, Becca!"

"And leave the blouse!" the security guard bellowed after them.

They rushed out the door into the salesroom. People stared. The salesclerk with the smock and the sensible shoes stood outside the dressing room, arms folded across her chest. Marne waited beside her.

"Close the door," Becca said.

The clerk pushed the louvered door shut. "We're out here," she said warningly with a glance at Marne.

"She's a little shy," Marne whispered.

"Ha!" scoffed the clerk, snatching up the blouse that Becca held out from a crack in the door. "Shy as a fox," she added.

Marne bit her lip. *Sly, you mean, you ignorant fool!* she wanted to retort. But she kept quiet, recalling one of Yitz's sermons: *"Who is wise? He who remains silent."*

It took all of Marne's effort to hold her head high as they walked through the store with the security guard and the clerk following. Nobody could miss the obvious; they had been questioned and accused of stealing, and they were probably set free on some technicality. It was like a tableau, people stopping to stare, some teenagers laughing as they passed. A boy called out, "Way to go!"

Outside in the mall Marne turned to Becca. Her face looked flushed, her features frozen, as if she would never speak to Marne again. "Look, Becca, I'm sorry. I lost track of time. I had no idea you'd walk out with those clothes on."

"Why didn't you come back? You said you'd come back in ten minutes!"

"I never said that. I told you to come and get me. I

assumed you'd pick out some things you liked and have the clerk hold them."

"Why didn't you come sooner? What were you doing?"

"I lost track of time, I told you. Hasn't that ever happened to you?"

"No! That policeman was grilling me for half an hour. He made me feel like a criminal. He was going to take me to the station, put me in jail."

"He was bluffing," Marne snapped. "They don't put kids in jail."

"Yes, they do. They take them to the station and call their parents."

"Well, he didn't tell your dad. He didn't leave a message even though he started to. So he must have believed you in the end."

"All those people looked at me as if I was a criminal!" Becca went on. "That just shows you, I should have gone to camp. I wish I had. I'm sorry I stayed here."

"I'm sorry I came!" Marne snapped. "Look, things happen. That doesn't mean you have to fall apart!"

"I'm not falling apart. I'm just saying you shouldn't have left me there, just because you wanted to be with that boy."

"Oh, so it's the boy that's really bothering you."

"I don't care if you're boy-crazy. I just want to go home."

"Boy-crazy?" Marne gave a laugh. "Come on, let's finish our shopping."

"I don't feel like shopping now."

Marne reached into her bag for the list. "We have to get this stuff for your mother. I promised."

Becca stood motionless, her arms folded across her chest.

"Okay," Marne said. "I'll find out where that crafts store is for the beads and the glitter and the ribbons. I can get a bathing suit for Elias down there at the beach shop, and there's a pharmacy . . ."

By the time Chaya drove up to meet them, Marne had assembled everything but the pacifier for Bennie and the beach towels. "They ran out of those beach towels you wanted, but they'll get more next week," Marne said as they got into the car.

Becca, silent, climbed into the backseat beside little Yossi and the baby in his car seat.

"And I couldn't find a pacifier," Marne added. She hoped Becca wouldn't start to complain, accusing her, maybe even crying again.

"We can probably find some old ones," Chaya said. "I had half a dozen. They get lost under the sofa cushions and in the oddest places. It's okay, Marne. Thanks for trying." Chaya gave her a quick smile. "We had a good day," she went on, driving fast and intently, as usual. "Bennie's checkup was excellent, Yossi has grown nearly two inches since the last checkup, and we even had time to stop for ice cream. Did you guys get a snack? Are you hungry?"

"I had a smoothie," Marne said. In a moment they would launch into it—sitting together with a boy, a date. Had she planned it in advance? Chaya would be suspicious. Here she was, in charge of Marne, who ran off meeting boys on the sly. And poor Becca, caught by the police, treated like a common criminal, all because Marne abandoned her so selfishly, just out for her own fun. . . . Marne could imagine the crisis.

Becca said nothing, and Marne turned to glance at her, but she swiftly looked away, biting the strands of her hair.

"So, what did you buy, Becca?" Chaya asked, glancing at Becca in the rearview mirror.

"Nothing."

"Nothing! But I thought . . ."

Marne held her breath.

"I didn't find anything appropriate," Becca said stiffly.

"Oh? Did you go to that boutique? We always find something there."

"Everything was sleeveless or too low-cut," Becca said testily. "Not *tznius*. I'll wait and spend my birthday money in the fall."

"You're quite a person," said her mother, beaming.

When they got home, everyone was in a mood. Jonathan was scowling, his hair standing on end. "The phone never stopped ringing!" he shouted. "And Dad won't come out of his office. I had to lock Nissim in his room, because I gave him a time-out and he wouldn't stay."

Nissim, in the middle of a tantrum, was banging on his bedroom door. "Becca, go let him out," Chaya commanded. Furious, she strode over to Jonathan, fist on her hip. "Don't you ever, ever lock him in again, do you hear me?"

"What was I supposed to do?"

"You were supposed to behave like a responsible person, that's what!" Chaya yelled. "Imagine, locking a child in. Anything could have happened!"

The twins had spilled liquid Jell-O onto the sofa in the family room, then attempted to clean it with cleanser and a steel wool pad. Bits of steel wool clung to the wet red stain. Esti, terrified, was sobbing at her mother's feet. Elias peered out from behind the couch, yelling, "I didn't do it! Not me!"

Marne took it all in, still stung by Becca's anger, the cop, the whole incident. She'd been so thrilled to be with Jeff, to have a normal afternoon, almost a real date. Was that so much to ask for? And now this.

For the first time, Chaya seemed completely immobilized, standing in the middle of a tempest. Little Bennie, perched on her hip, started to cry. The only one who seemed unaffected by the chaos was Yossi. Marne turned to him and said firmly, "Yossi, go get that extra blanket out of Becca's closet—the plaid one. We'll put it on the couch over the mess. Elias, you help him. Esti, come here, honey. I brought you some ribbons. Let's put them in your hair."

Chaya gave her a long look before she set the baby down and fled along the hall to Yitz's study. "Why haven't you paid attention to—" she began.

"I'm in the middle of a crisis here," Marne heard him say, his voice rising. "Amy Switzer has to have surgery. She asked me to—" Then the door closed, and Marne was left alone with the kids, aware that they were all looking at her. Bennie sat on the floor, his pants having slid down around his ankles. He was starting to pucker up for a good howl.

Marne took a deep breath and managed a smile. "There's something for everybody," she said. "Elias, here's your new bathing suit. Nissim, I got you the glue for your model. You have to be sure to put the cap back on tight. Yossi, I got you some Superman stickers."

"What about Bennie?" Esti said challengingly, her arms crossed over her chest in imitation of her mother.

"Oh, his is the best," Marne said, grinning. She reached into the bag and brought out a pair of tiny suspenders, red, white, and blue–striped. She scooped up the baby, sat down on the floor with him in her lap, and snapped the suspenders into place. All the kids watched, entranced, as Bennie, some glimmer of understanding lighting up his face, took off across the room and scurried back again and threw himself into Marne's arms. He giggled. Marne held him close for a moment, blew a kiss onto his silky hair.

"Where's Jonathan's present?" Nissim asked. His brother gave him a swift swipe on the side of the head. The kids all froze, their eyes fully upon her.

Marne sighed. She had bought herself a new CD by Tris and the Triplets. She reached into her bag for the CD and held it out to Jonathan. He glanced at it, then looked away. "Sorry," he said. "I don't listen to that kind of music."

There was a small sink in the family room, designed as a bar, with glass shelves on either side and a mirror wall. The children lined up to wash before supper. Becca held Baby Bennie while Nissim poured water from the special pitcher onto the baby's little hands. Bennie smiled and beamed as he lisped part of the blessing: *"Baruch atah Adonai . . ."* He laughed and kicked his plump legs, and Marne found herself echoing the blessing in her mind. She watched from a distance, as always, waiting for everyone to be seated before she took her place. *Their habits aren't my habits,* she told herself. She wished she could have spent more time with Jeff; he understood what she was going through, the control, the obsession with every detail, from the morning hand washing to the evening prayer.

Marne was closest to the telephone when it rang, and she hurried to answer.

"Marne, is that you? So glad to catch you. I called before. Nobody home. I guess they're keeping you busy. Are you having fun?"

"Oh, yes, Mom," Marne said with a quick flashback

over the day and Becca's angry tears. "It's great." She wondered whether the icy sarcasm came through all the way to Paris. "How about you, Mom?"

"Oh, everything's fine, I guess. Busy, busy. Some frustrations. Upheaval here, with lots of gossip and conjecture. We're all disgusted and upset. One of the production assistants ran off with Pierre's major new design for the season. Everyone trusted him. He'd been with Pierre for seven years. *C'est la vie,*" she said in a breezy tone, quite unlike her usual self. "How was your day?" her mom asked, an obvious afterthought. "Fun?"

"Becca and I went to the mall," Marne said. She lowered her voice. The kids were rushing to sit down, with the usual commotion. "I met this boy from San Diego and ran into him at the mall. He's a neat guy, surfs and is really into sports."

"Your dad would like that, wouldn't he?"

"His name's Jeff. He's part Jewish."

"Oh, Chaya and Yitz will get off on that!"

"I invited him over for *Shabbos* dinner."

Her mom gave a quick, throaty laugh. "Sounds like a good way to discourage him."

"Really?" Marne grasped the edge of the counter.

Now they were all seated at the table, waiting. Yitz was passing around the platter of meatballs and spaghetti, the tray of toasted French bread. "You think?"

"I *know*."

"Okay. Well, I'm glad you mentioned it. We're just about ready to eat dinner."

"I figured. Marne, call your father. He says he hasn't heard from you."

"I will. My cell phone was broken. I just got it fixed."

"When is Kim coming?"

"Three more days. I can't wait!"

"Give her my love. Say hello to her folks for me. When I get back, we should have them over again for a barbecue."

"Okay. Thanks, Mom."

"Give my love to Carole and everyone. Next time I'll talk to her. Don't want to intrude on her supper."

As Marne replaced the receiver, she was overwhelmed with longing, though she couldn't define what it was she longed for. They hadn't had a barbecue in over a year. Last time Kim and her family came over was two summers ago. Was she homesick for her parents? Her friends? No—Kim was coming to Hawaii in just three days, and Kim was her best friend. It would be wonderful. Then—what?

Marne went to the table and sat down at her place beside Becca, opposite Jonathan. They had waited for her, the food on their plates getting cold.

"Mom says hello," Marne said, feeling embarrassed, empty.

Chaya passed the platter to Marne. "I'm so glad your mother called. You must miss her," she said.

"I do," Marne said, knowing it was a lie. What she missed was the comfortable feeling of knowing who she was, of fitting in. Here, she was still a guest, and their politeness was every bit as unsettling as Becca's moody silence.

Evenings here were catch-up time, private time, as Chaya put it. No television, with its prime-time shows filled with sexual innuendo, the alarming news broadcasts, or movies about killers and vampires and drug addicts. The boys studied Torah and commentaries with Yitz. He told them stories from the Bible, about kings and their loyal subjects, adding drama to the telling with wide gestures that held Elias and Nissim entranced. Sometimes even Baby Bennie sat in his high chair as if he, too, were learning, while he picked Cheerios off his tray. Chaya would take Esti and Yossi and sometimes Becca, and they traced Hebrew letters onto white construction paper, using an array of colored markers, glitter, and other decorations. Their finished artwork was displayed on the kitchen wall. Then Marne would remember the days when she and Jody and their mom would spend an entire morning gathering "stuff," driftwood and pebbles, sea glass and junk hardware that they called "lost treasure," using it to create collages that Mom later propped up on the window seat, where everyone could admire them.

This was the time Marne often went out to the patio, where she sat on an old wicker bench under the banyan tree and played her guitar. Now she sat there with her guitar, looking up at the stars, softly singing camp songs, popular songs, and several of her own. Her voice did not, could not, match the depth of her feelings, a longing for something she could not name. The Hawaiian night was almost too beautiful to bear, unless there was someone to share it with.

She became aware of a presence, some unseen force, an invisible observer.

Quickly she turned and saw a fleeting shadow at the window behind her.

Jonathan. Somehow she knew it was he, having

briefly escaped his father's lesson, coming to hear the music.

Quick tears sprang to her eyes, tears of anger and resentment. She wanted to scream at Jonathan, to accuse him. *Coward! How dare you run away from me, from the music? You have this talent, and it's all going to waste. Don't you know I'd give anything to sing like that? To compose like that?*

She put the guitar away. It was no use. She'd never be able to talk to Jonathan, or if she did, he wouldn't hear her.

chapter THIRTEEN

Yitz, standing by the mirror wall in the living room, loomed like an Old World monk in his black clothes and black hat, his beard vibrating with his voice. His tone was soft, sometimes rising in power, and he offered few gestures, unlike preachers on TV who waved their arms and expressed wide-ranging emotions on their faces. No, Yitz was calm and quiet, neither urging nor arguing. He simply told it the way he saw it, and the people listened, some with their arms folded over their chests, some nodding and murmuring, like Marjorie, the woman sitting beside Marne. She seemed to have sought Marne out with her smile and her hand extended.

"Good *Shabbos,* my dear!"

Old Sol sat with his legs apart, as if the folding chair could not quite sustain him. He alternately nodded and shook his head, but slightly, so as not to appear to be taking issue with the rabbi's remarks. But Marne had heard him, his singsongy accented voice: "After the Holocaust, who believes anymore in God?"

"The Lord reigns, indeed the world is firmly established that it shall not falter; He will judge the people with righteousness. . . ."

Justice and fairness, that is what's expected from God, isn't it? Justice and fairness. "He has revealed His justice before the eyes of the nations. . . ." Justice, justice, shall you pursue. Yitz knew how to milk words, to extract every essence from them, elaborating, embroidering, like a jazz musician improvising on a theme.

Marjorie turned to Marne and whispered, "I heard how you helped Chaya at the *taharah*! How wonderful."

Marne searched for something to say. "Have you ever done it?"

"Oh, my dear, no. I'm not cut out for that. Of course, I believe in doing a *mitzvah,* but . . . well, every morning I go out on my porch and I feed the birds."

"I see," Marne whispered.

"And I say, '*Shalom,* birds! It's another beautiful day, *baruch Hashem*!' "

Marjorie gave Marne a searching look.

"Birds are very interesting creatures," said Marne. "I—have you been coming here long? To *Shabbos*?"

"Nearly five years," Marjorie said stoutly. "They are like family to me. Can you imagine how many chickens Chaya cooks in a year? That woman is a saint."

"So, you became religious," Marne stated.

"Well, I light a candle every *Shabbos* that I'm here. I say the blessings for food, but . . . religious? I believe in God. That's it. And now I'm not lonely."

Yitz was talking about the psalm: "When the wicked thrive like grass and all evildoers prosper . . . what is their final recompense?" Marne's eyes felt heavy. It was all too confusing. The rational mind could not deal with the inconsistencies.

Beside Yitz stood Jonathan in his dark suit and that large, incongruous hat. Jonathan bobbed and swayed as he pronounced each word in a lively duet with his father. Nissim, behind him, first struggled to keep up, then dashed off to play with the twins. And Marne breathed a sigh of relief; at least here was one normal kid. When did they change and become such sullen, pale, and intense little men?

Jeff said he'd come. Marne repeated the memory of that morning, when he watched her jog, a stopwatch in his hand, shouting when she broke her own record by seven seconds. She was steaming like a racehorse, exhilarated.

The sweat layering her body and her face made her feel powerful, like an athlete coming in for the final turn. She didn't want to stop running. The endorphins must have kicked in. Or—was it something else? Was it seeing Jeff's grin and the way he held out his arms to give her a victory hug? He had held her, and she could feel his cool skin against her hot, throbbing body. Cool and powerful and so very comforting.

When she got back to the house, Becca was gathering equipment for day camp, speaking in a cool, disinterested tone, her eyes averted. "Mom wants you to do some necklaces with the girls today. Here's a box of stuff."

"Fine," said Marne. "Look, Becca, how long are you going to stay mad?"

"I'm not mad."

"Have it your way." Marne drew closer. Becca stepped away. "I invited Jeff to *Shabbos* dinner," Marne said. "Are you going to be nice to him, at least?"

Becca gave her a disparaging look. "Whatever."

Jeff said he wanted to come, would like to come, would probably come.

Marne had felt the flurry of Sabbath preparations more deeply than ever before. It was her fifth Friday night here, and she knew the pattern and accommodated to it

188

without allowing herself to blend completely. She thought of old Sol, of the many professed unbelievers who sat here on Friday nights or at the run-down dump of a hotel on Saturday mornings, who came to listen and to complain, to argue and to insist: "Rabbi, if there is a God, and if He is all powerful and all good, how come . . ."

Babies die in their cribs. Houses burn down. An airplane lands in a suburb and crashes into someone's bedroom, slicing the whole house in half. Why? Who ordained it? Who allows it? And the shattered remains—who will repair them?

Marne found herself singing along with Yitz and the others the chorus of the Sabbath song: "*Lecha dodi, likrat kallah*. . . . Come, my beloved, to greet the Sabbath bride." She was learning the words.

Everyone stood up, and so did Marne. She glanced out the window, wondering whether Jeff was standing there, just waiting for the right moment to enter. He would be a little shy. Maybe he'd be holding something, a small bouquet of flowers or some candy, as his dad would have told him was appropriate. Or maybe he'd just bring his smile and that magnificent tan, his hair curly, not too short, not too long. What would he wear? A white shirt, maybe? Or something cool, something sporty.

She was wearing the white gauze skirt she'd picked up at the mall and a peach-colored T-shirt with a sheer white blouse over it, tied at the waist. She wore her favorite silver barrette to keep her hair back from her face, but full down around her shoulders, because Jeff had said he loved her hair, loved the color and the touch. He said she smelled like strawberries. That was bold. Nobody had ever talked to her that way. And he—he smelled of the sea and of cocoa, from the sunblock he used, and she'd wanted to say that he smelled like chocolate, but that would be too provocative, so she only smiled and said, "I'm glad you like strawberries."

The silent prayer commenced, and Marne, standing with the others, read the words and tried to let herself feel them. ". . . God of Abraham, God of Isaac, God of Jacob . . ." From repetition, the words now slid easily into her mind, like a passing scene. She did not believe in ritualized prayer. Even Yitz had told her, if you want to talk to God, just have your own conversation. Why should she recite words that some stranger had dictated two thousand years ago? That was his prayer, not hers. Hers was simple. *Make Jeff come tonight. Make him like me. Make him come here, and then make him ask me to take a walk on the beach with him. . . .*

Chaya and Yitz would bar the door—wouldn't they? Or they'd keep him talking, keep him there with some clever tactic. They'd never let her out with him to watch the moonlight glisten on the water, to feel the sweet breeze and his lips against hers. He had not kissed her. Not yet. *Please,* she prayed silently, *let him kiss me. If you are there, God, prove it! Make him come tonight. Let him take me out to the sand and let him kiss me.*

Yitz, now engrossed in his sermon, clutched the cloth belt that was wound around his waist. It hung down past the hem of his long black coat. Holiness, he said, did not mean shutting yourself away to pray and meditate in solitude all day. "No, we must participate in the mundane, everyday world, the working world. We must transform the world into a place where God can dwell."

And Marne wondered at that word *mundane,* wondered how many in the disparate, scruffy little group sitting on hard folding chairs even knew the word. *Mundane.*

"But isn't God everywhere?" asked Shirley. She was alarmingly thin and her scalp showed through badly tinted hair. "Why should we have to create a place for Him?"

"Good question . . ." Yitz launched into an explanation, and Marne looked at her watch. Maybe Jeff decided to skip the service and show up for dinner. That was okay, too. People did that here. Everybody was welcome, no matter how briefly, how unexpectedly. Because they just might pick up a *mitzvah,* an idea, a glimmer of *Yiddish-keit*—Jewishness, but more, it meant the feeling, the taste, the smell, the sound, and the joy of being Jewish. For Yitz and Chaya and the kids, being Jewish was an entirely unique and elevated condition.

Then why, Marne wanted to know, were Jews persecuted all the time? Why were they hated?

"They hate us," old Sol would grumble.

Marjorie took up the litany. "Oy, yes, they do. We can kiss their you-know-what, and they still hate us."

"Now, now, let's lose that negativity!" Chaya would burst in, cheerful as a camp counselor facing a disaster. She nodded to Jonathan. Jonathan started a song without words, a *niggun,* just a simple pattern of five or six notes, repeated endlessly, and then came the slapping at the table, the voices thin or strong, off-key or right on: *"Ya-da-da-da-da-ya-dee-da-dum!"*

Not here yet, Jeff was probably on the way now. He'd get here in time for dinner. He'd sit down beside her, and they would have their own secret conversation with their eyes. Maybe his foot would touch hers ever so lightly under the table.

This time Marne had joined in the Friday-afternoon transformation with new energy. She had done all her chores, helping to wipe down the counters, snapping plastic wrap over the platters and bowls of prepared food—salads, marinated fish, melon balls, chunks of cake and brownies made yesterday, the bulk of them saved at great effort and with multiple threats and promises: "They're for *Shabbos*! You can have a tiny piece now. We're saving them for *Shabbos*!"

A few hours before *Shabbos,* the transformation began. Chaya seemed to cast off her drill-sergeant mode and move into a slower, more contemplative existence. Her features seemed smoother, her hands quiet. She bathed, and her skin smelled of fresh lavender. She wore a long, flowered skirt and a silky blouse, and a silk ribbon was wound around her head, as if the perfect wig were not a wig at all. Her lips glistened with a pale coral lipstick, and she had rubbed pale green shadow onto her eyelids, so that her eyes looked luminous and large.

Everyone moved with a sense of purpose. The clock was ticking! *Shabbos* would arrive with or without their notice—better finish everything, clean it up, put it away, organize.

Jonathan, assertive and sober, tracked his dad taking innumerable trips from the van to the house, bringing in food, soft drinks, extra chairs, books, and toys. The living room became a small lecture hall, with added folding chairs and a couple of card tables against the side walls. These were covered with plastic cloths and laid with paper cups, drinks, and a platter of cookies. Several bottles of wine went into the refrigerator. It was Becca's job to arrange blossoms in a vase on the card table. Nissim, his hair slicked down from his shower and *tzitzis* swinging from under his white dress shirt, was in charge of soda. Businesslike, he lugged the big bottles of 7UP and Coke from the kitchen to the card tables, where they stood dripping with condensation. Esti and Elias were in charge of guarding the cookies that everyone ate before dinner, after blessing the wine. Strange, wasn't it? Cookies before dinner?

Yossi set out the napkins and ran around picking up derelict toys, tossing them into a huge toy bin and yelling, "Clean up! Clean up and put away!" The greatest difficulty was keeping the four younger children clean and ready. Marne was responsible for Bennie and Esti. For

Bennie, it was a game. First she had to catch him as he scooted across the floor, laughing and shrieking. Then she scooped him up and carried him to the kitchen sink, where he insisted on having suds, which he patted and blew until Marne was soaked. Marne dressed him in fresh clothes, a *kippa* clipped onto his curls, and put him into his swing, hanging in the doorway, while she supervised Esti in the bathtub. She washed Esti's hair and let it dry in the warm air, falling into taffy-colored curls all around her face. Esti liked to be rubbed in a huge bath towel and rocked like a baby. Marne sang to her while she rocked, then tickled her a little to make her laugh and pull away.

What would Jeff think of them? Jonathan with his black suit and outlandish hat, his grim handshake. Becca rushing around being the little homemaker, making sure everyone had enough food. The twins dancing and shouting and jumping. Would he think this was a madhouse? Would he take one look and want to leave? Would he ask Marne to come with him to the mall to get some sushi or a pizza, and then would she have the guts to walk out and go with him? And how could Yitz and Chaya complain? After all, she wasn't religious.

The salads and the fish plates were removed. Esti,

195

Elias, and Nissim handed out fresh forks for everyone. Becca brought a stack of plastic plates from the kitchen. And Marne, miserable and aching, took the huge platter of meat from Chaya and brought it into the dining room, where the table had been expanded to full length, with another table with folding chairs resting snugly against one another, twenty or so people waiting for their food, singing beneath Yitz's spirited basso voice, and Marne knew he wasn't coming, wasn't coming, and the evening would be dismal as before, with long stories and droning and clapping and that final prayer for the food, when her eyes would start to close. . . . But it wasn't so. She felt it first, a presence, an intuitive knowledge. She set the platter down carefully right in front of Marjorie, who always piled her plate high, since she lived on welfare and pretended to be full so that she could take the leftovers home in a little bag.

Marne set the platter down and turned. And there he was, with that smile.

chapter FOURTEEN

He kissed her.

It didn't happen exactly as Marne had planned. All through dinner, Nissim rushed over to Jeff's chair, and the boy didn't leave Jeff's side for an instant. It was pure hero worship, Nissim gazing up at Jeff with longing and admiration in his eyes. "What a neat watch!" Nissim exclaimed, touching Jeff's wrist. "What neat sneakers!" They happened to be black. "Want to see my fishes? They're Arnold and Tanya, Marne helped me buy Tanya, she's the wife." Nissim offered Jeff seconds of everything. He prepared a dessert plate for him, piled with brownies, cake, and fruit.

Marne, watching, felt a proprietary pleasure, as if Jeff belonged to her and she was sharing him, showing him off. Everyone could see how wonderful he was, fielding questions, smiling, paying attention.

He spoke to Marjorie and Sol and Shirley, and he laughed at Sol's silly, creaking jokes. He praised the food,

197

making Chaya smile and flip her hair back over her shoulder. He thanked Becca for making the brownies, his favorite food in the world, he said. When Baby Bennie, leaning out too far, crashed out of his high chair, Jeff was the first one on his feet. He scooped up the baby, swung him high, and rocked him down again, so that Bennie chortled and forgot his fall.

"I had a great time," Jeff said when Marne walked with him to the door.

"Looks like it," Marne said with a smile. "You're the last to leave." Behind her in the quiet house, Chaya was putting the little kids to bed. Yitz had gone out back with the trash bags, probably stopping to enjoy the night sky. All the guests were gone.

At the front door he took her hand and drew her close. And then he kissed her.

Gradually Becca thawed out. It began in the kitchen later that week, while they were rolling dough for homemade pizza.

"There's a pizza place right by our house," Marne said, "just across from the beach. I go there all the time and watch the guy tossing up the dough."

"Does he always catch it?" Becca asked.

"Sure," said Marne. "So do I."

The other kids jostled in close, excited. "Can you really do it?" they clamored. "Do it! Show us, Marne!"

Grinning, Marne grabbed a clump of dough, smacked it down flat on the board with her hand, and for good measure gave it a few more slaps. She pried up the dough and let it circle from her fingers, around and around, then deftly she tossed it a little to the side and upward, like a Frisbee.

"Whoa!" yelled the kids, laughing and stamping as Marne caught the dough platter on her fingertips. "Do it again! Again!"

Again she let it fly, this time higher, and again, higher.

"What's going on?" Chaya's imperious voice broke through the chorus. And as Marne's eyes flickered away for an instant, the dough came sailing down, landing squarely on Nissim's head.

Everyone froze. Nissim rolled his eyes. Then he began to giggle, his stomach heaving, until he was doubled over on the floor. Screams of laughter filled the kitchen, summoning Yitz, who instantly caught the contagious hilarity. The kids fell over one another laughing. Becca grabbed

Marne's arm, gasping, "You are tooo funny, Marne. Oh, Marne! You're the best!"

That night they made plans. "A cookout," Marne suggested. "Like camp."

"We can make s'mores," Becca said.

On the beach in front of the house, piles of sea rocks provided natural campfire pits. "We can make tongs out of sticks," Marne said. "We used to do that at camp and roast our s'mores over the fire."

"It has to be dark," Becca said. "That's part of the fun."

Marne agreed. "I like to watch the fire."

"Bring your guitar."

"Of course."

"When can we do it?"

"We have to get the stuff," Marne said. "Graham crackers and chocolate bars. We have kosher marshmallows."

"Thursdays my mom does her big shopping. We'll give her a list."

"Sure." They were sitting on their beds. Marne reached for her guitar and played a few chords.

"Teach me that song again," Becca said. "About the kookaburra."

They sang it twice. Then Becca said, "We never had

songs like that at our camp. They were always about *mitzvos* and *Moshiach* and stuff like that."

"Well, it was a religious camp, wasn't it?"

Becca nodded. "We did have cookouts, though," she said. "Actually, I didn't mean it when I said I wished I'd gone back. I wanted to stay here with you."

"That's okay," Marne said.

Becca got under her covers, and Marne, wide awake, reached for one of her summer reading books. She read until soft sounds of sleep came from Becca. Marne got up quietly and made her way to the kitchen.

"Hey! I thought you girls were fast asleep." Chaya stood there, a large towel under her arm, searching through her bag for something.

"Becca's asleep," Marne said. "I was reading. Don't we have some of that pizza left over?"

"In the fridge. You can microwave it. Listen, I'll see you later."

"Where are you going?" Marne found the pizza and a paper plate and punched in the microwave timer.

"Out," Chaya said curtly.

The microwave oven sounded. Marne took out the pizza and cut it into two. "Want some?" she offered.

Chaya shook her head. "I just brushed my teeth."

Now Marne saw that Chaya's face glowed as if it had been scrubbed, and she wore a long white shirt that reached far below her knees. Chaya gazed at her for a long moment. "Maybe," she said, "you'd like to come with me. I'm going for a swim. It's up the road about six miles, a private little cove. That is, nobody's ever there. I've made it my *mikveh.*"

"What?"

"Ritual bath. A monthly thing, you know, after my period. A spiritual cleansing."

"Ah. I see." But of course, Marne didn't.

"Sometimes Kalima comes with me, or my friend Gloria, but they're not available and . . . I don't want to wait."

"I see," Marne repeated.

"Because until a woman has done this immersion, she and her husband can't . . . can't have relations."

The words popped into Marne's mind. *Strange relations.* Her heart leaped with embarrassment. There were so many questions she did not want to ask, answers she didn't really want to hear, though on the other hand she was prodded by curiosity.

"What would I do?" she asked.

"Nothing," replied Chaya. "Just hang out. Maybe go for a swim."

Marne hastily finished the pizza, wiped her hands, and said, grinning, "Hey, I'm game!"

An occasional splatter of oncoming headlights brought Marne back to reality. The dark night, the nearly silent road, and the hushed sounds of the waves made Marne feel as if she had been launched into another zone, another time. They sat on the sand, she and Chaya, talking like girlfriends, for without the children around her, Chaya seemed young and carefree. She talked about growing up in Florida, uncomfortable with the ostentatious life her parents craved.

"A new car every few years, usually a snazzy convertible." Chaya laughed and hugged the large bath towel around her body. "All I wanted to do was go to classes and make jewelry. I had a small kiln, and I made enamel bracelets and earrings out of copper and baked them in it."

"I didn't know that," Marne said. She smiled to herself. "You and Mom are both into the arts in different ways."

"I always loved color and design. So I applied to several

art schools, but I realized I'd probably need something more practical. I wanted to see California, so I applied to UCLA to take courses in child development. I figured I could teach art and also have my own small studio."

"Did you like UCLA? I think maybe I'll go there," Marne said, "unless I go away to school."

Chaya shook her head. "It got pretty stressful. I stopped short of just one semester. I guess that was pretty stupid. But by then I had made friends with a lot of people, *frum* people, and it changed my life. Also, I had met Yitz."

"And he was from New York, wasn't he?"

Chaya nodded. "It was *bashert*. Destiny." She leaned back, her elbows on the sand, her gaze up at the stars. "He had been in this group for a couple of years already. He wore a black hat and coat, pretty weird on the UCLA campus. It took guts, but he did it. He was the first *baal teshuva* I ever knew, and I was flabbergasted, thought he was so weird, until he started to talk to me. Then he seemed so—well, gentle and strong, both together. He had to buck everyone, his friends, his parents, and his family, to get into that new space, to look for God and to make that decision to be observant."

"Like born-again Christians," Marne mused.

"Something like that," Chaya said. "His folks aren't the least bit religious. In fact, they have a Christmas tree. His mom says it doesn't mean anything. It's just a fun holiday that doesn't have to be religious." She shrugged. "So, Yitz was searching, and he met these students, *frum* kids, and the rabbis, and he began to study and to go regularly to services. He and some of his buddies had built a *sukkah* on campus that fall. I ran into it—literally." Chaya laughed. "I was rushing to class and suddenly I banged into this little hut, and then I saw the sign welcoming Jewish students to come have a light meal in the *sukkah*. I was starving; it was way past lunchtime, and I hadn't eaten. So I went in and pretty soon I was surrounded by people, all of them so friendly! They served grape juice and cheese and crackers and cake, and before I knew it, I'd been there for a whole hour and had made plans to come to their service the next Friday night."

"And you were hooked," Marne stated. "They tried to convert you. To suck you in." Marne heard the bitterness in her voice, but Chaya only smiled.

"Yes, well, that's what they say. But I wasn't hooked, as you call it. I wanted it. It took a while to realize what I'd been missing. It was gradual, and yet it felt as if I was coming home to something in my own past, in my own

205

soul. Does that sound corny? I began seeing things differently. I felt connected. Before, I was just floating around. Now I was with people who wanted the same things I did, just a simple, good life. I was with people who really want to improve the world. Holy people. I know it sounds strange these days, that word, *holy.* But it's beautiful."

"When did you and Yitz decide to get married?"

"Well, that was the problem. We couldn't actually date, the way the secular kids do. We looked at each other, sort of from afar. Then we started doing projects together for the group, spending time. Of course, it became apparent that something was going on between us. We talked it over and decided not to see each other—that is, except in the group, until we could really make a commitment."

"Is that why you left school before graduation?" Marne asked.

"Oh, no," Chaya said, shaking her head emphatically. "I wanted to get my degree. But some of my teachers made it so difficult. I remember, especially, the professor in my sociology class gave me a D on my term paper, because he said it was filled with dogma and superstitious nonsense. In other words, religion. He was—livid. Said I was supposed to be objective and scientific. Well, I had footnotes, of course, and quotes from many sources. . . ."

"So you quit because of that?"

"Well, I'm not proud of it," Chaya said. "I should have stayed, but I was feeling confused and overwhelmed. I always figured I'd go back for my degree." She gave Marne a sidelong glance and a smile. "Maybe when the kids are grown, I will."

They sat quietly. Marne looked at the stars, the black sky, the white foam from the waves. Chaya sighed. "It was probably a mistake to let it affect me so much. I was weak."

"You were tired."

"Yes. So, what do you think you'll do after high school?" Chaya asked.

"I don't know. Maybe study music. There's a great music school in Boston."

"Would you teach? You're wonderful with children. They adore you."

"I don't know. Maybe." A quick recollection of Jody flashed into her mind. It hurt, but with the pain there was something else, almost a sense of peace. Memories washed over her—the times Jody was a pest, jumping on the bed, playing ball in the house, screaming with laughter, and then the memories of sitting close together on the sofa, watching TV, holding Jody's hand if something scary came onto the screen, and the special smell of her little sister, something impossible to describe.

Chaya stood up, pulling the towel closer around her shoulders. "I think you'll be good at whatever you decide," she said. "You're a good worker. Committed. Like the *taharah;* you didn't quit." Chaya dropped the towel and stood on the sand in her long white shirt, like an old-fashioned nightshirt, and she pulled the scarf from her head. Her hair, short and spiky, looked shiny in the moonlight. "I have to go in," she said softly, "without clothes. Naked."

"Oh," said Marne. "I won't look at you."

"Thanks. But when I come out . . ."

"I can hand you a towel without looking at you."

"Okay," said Chaya. "Afterward, maybe you'll want to swim. It's lovely here."

Marne turned her back to the ocean, and she listened to the rustle of the leafy banyan tree at the water's edge, to the crackle of seawater against the rocks and the *whoosh* as it pulled back from the shore.

Marne glanced over to the water, where Chaya's head

208

emerged for a moment, then she ducked down again, three times. Marne had worn her bikini under her pants and shirt. She walked to the edge of the sand, unbuttoning her shirt as she went. She longed to plunge into those waves in the darkness, to submerge in the water and then float, looking up at the stars.

A scream. Panic. "Marne! Oh, oh my God!"

Marne ran into the water up to her knees. Chaya came toward her, staggering and clutching her side, and to her horror, Marne saw blood between her fingers. Chaya sank down on the sand. Her form was white as marble in the moonlight, except for the blooming red stain that lay across her breast and flowed down into the sand.

chapter FIFTEEN

Marne was not aware of thinking, only of the flashes of light accosting her. She felt blinded by the white tips of the waves, Chaya's white body, Chaya's teeth gleaming as she gasped, "Marne, Marne . . . it hurts! Something . . . bit me. Out there . . . something."

Questions streamed into Marne's mind—were there sharks in Hawaii? She stared at Chaya's nude body, the blood seeping from a gash that ran from under her breast to her back, as if she had been sliced with a sword. Marne took Chaya's white shirt and pressed it gently against the wound. In Chaya's bag she found a packet of wipes—how many dozens of times she had seen Chaya reach for those moist wipes for sticky hands and grubby faces. *Antiseptic,* the words rang through Marne's mind, *clean the wound, keep her warm, because* . . . Marne gulped in air, swallowed down her fear. She knew about death now. It seemed so long ago that she and Chaya and Kalima had washed and dressed that cold corpse, and now Chaya lay on the sand, her body curled in pain. All these thoughts raced through Marne's mind in a moment as she bent down, took Chaya's arm, and said in a firm tone, new to her own ears, "Get up, Chaya. We have to get you to a doctor. *Now.*"

"I . . . I feel so . . . dizzy."

"Don't talk. Just come to the car. I know the way."

"Where . . . ?"

"That little emergency clinic by the supermarket." Docs in the box, her dad called those small clinics. Life-savers. "Chaya, don't worry."

Marne pulled off her shirt and wrapped it around Chaya, leaving one sleeve empty. Then she laid the beach towel around Chaya's shoulders. "Come on, Chaya, you have to walk to the car. Lean on me."

"I'm bleeding!"

"Don't worry. You'll be fine."

"Where's my bag?"

"I've got it. We have to go, Chaya."

The car felt unfamiliar, a huge bulky beast. Marne had never driven a van, never manipulated a gearshift down beside the seat. She pulled; nothing moved. At last she pushed in the handle and managed to spin the car around—too fast, so that Chaya lurched forward and cried out. Marne glanced at the towel, at the spreading stain of blood.

"I'm sorry, I'm sorry," Marne breathed. Slow down, her mind commanded. Slow down and think. Help her. *Help her!* She glanced over at her aunt, the slumping figure, pale lips moving wordlessly. Chaya's breathing was shallow and halting. *Shock,* Marne thought, reaching over to take Chaya's hand. It was damp and cold. "You're going to be okay," Marne said. "Don't worry. I'll get you to that clinic." Her voice was surprisingly calm, and now Marne understood the reason for the constant patter of nurses and teachers and relief workers; the human voice is like a human hand, reaching to give comfort and connection. "You're going to be fine. It's only a few minutes away."

She glanced at Chaya, who lay against the back of the seat now. Her face was pale, almost bluish in the meager light.

"Talk to me, Chaya," Marne said. "Is the pain bad?"

"So cold," Chaya whispered. She was trembling.

Marne pulled over, leaped from the van, groped in the

212

back, and pulled out the old beach blanket that the kids used as a tent, a fort, a place to lie on in the sand. Bits of sand struck Marne's face as she swiftly gave it a shake, jumped back into the car, and turned to Chaya.

"I'm going to put this around you," she murmured. "Don't worry, it won't touch your wound. You have to keep warm."

"Yes, okay," Chaya whispered obediently. "Thank you." She shook violently, pressed her lips together.

Marne sped to the intersection, just a few blocks from the house, but there was no time to go there, no time to waste. A small car skidded in front of her as she made a swift turn into the parking lot. "Damn it! Look out!" Marne exclaimed, her heart racing. She broke out in sweat across her neck and on her face. Her heart pounded as she pulled the van into a parking space. The bumper hit a curb. Chaya let out a cry.

"Sorry! Stay here!" Marne called out, jumping from the van. She ran to the clinic, the white door with a red cross painted on it; inside an elderly man in a white smock was tending to a boy lying on a cot. The boy was barefoot and wearing filthy shorts. On the floor beside him was a skateboard.

"Please, hurry!" Marne shouted. "My aunt's out in the car. She's been attacked by something in the ocean. Maybe a shark."

At the word *shark* the medic dropped the gauze bandage, hastily fastened it, and told the boy, "Go on, now. And stay off that skateboard!"

"She's in that blue van. Hurry!" Marne called, running out.

They helped Chaya out of the van, the doctor supporting her under one elbow. Marne rushed to her other side. Clumsily they made their way into the small clinic with its blazing bright lights. The doctor ripped a fresh paper covering from a roller and tossed it onto the cot. "Here, we'll lay her down," he said, panting. "Let's have a look. Hmmm. Oh, my, yes, quite a tear. Long, but not too deep, no organs affected. We'll have to give you an injection. Tetanus. Then we'll stitch you up."

"Stitches!" Marne cried.

"Clamps, actually. We don't sew flesh anymore. That's old-school." He nodded, smiling, disavowing his sparse white hair, the bony skull that pronounced an advanced age, and schooling done many decades ago.

Using cotton swabs and a yellow liquid, the doctor cleaned the wound several times. Tears slid from beneath

Chaya's closed eyelids; otherwise she was motionless. The doctor felt her pulse. "Could use a shot of Adrenalin," he murmured, and prepared the hypodermic.

Marne grimaced, and she took Chaya's hand in hers. She watched intently as color returned to Chaya's face. Chaya lifted her head and said, "Call Yitz."

"Now, you have to lie still for a while," said the doctor. He turned to Marne. "Want to use the phone to call your dad?"

"Sure," Marne said, not stopping to explain. Yitz answered immediately. He sounded sleepy. Marne told him everything, ending with, "We're at the clinic in the strip mall."

"I'll be right there," Yitz said. "Let me talk to Chaya."

Marne gave the phone to Chaya. "No," Chaya said. "Don't come. Stay with the children. I don't need you, Yitz. Marne's taking care of everything."

Out in the van once more, Marne realized with a jolt that she was wearing only her bikini. Chaya, dressed in Marne's shirt and wrapped in the beach towel, lay back half asleep, murmuring, "Thank God you were there, Marne. Thank God."

Marne's head throbbed, and her leg on the accelerator was shaking. For her, fear always came later. She had found Chaya's insurance card in her wallet and she gave all the information, her tone cool and unemotional. An emergency sent her into a command mode, but now that the crisis was over, she felt weak and sick.

"You did the right thing," the doctor had told Marne, patting her hand. "Now you look a little peaked yourself, young lady. Go home. Relax. Tell your dad to give you a shot of whiskey." He laughed. "That's an old folk remedy," he said. "Works every time." He filled a small plastic bag with ointment and a packet of tablets. "Antibiotic ointment," he explained. "And some painkillers if she needs 'em. Samples. Have your mom apply that ointment twice a day. And if she gets a fever or an infection, she'd better see a doctor right away."

She's not my mom, Marne started to say, but what was the point?

She turned the car into the driveway. Yitz, standing at the front window, rushed out. He reached for Chaya, and the moment her feet touched the ground, he took her up in his arms and carried her into the house. *Like a bride,* Marne thought.

A few minutes later Yitz came into the kitchen, where Marne sat, staring dully ahead. She was wrapped in a cotton robe she had found hanging from a hook on the

216

laundry room door. The robe felt comforting, as if she had been sick and was now beginning to get well.

"How about some tea?" Yitz asked.

She smiled. "The doctor prescribed whiskey."

"We don't have whiskey. But maybe a little wine," Yitz said. He went to the sideboard and brought back a bottle of red wine and two glasses. "It is appropriate, I think," he said. "We'll say a *l'chaim* and thank *Hashem* for having you there when Chaya needed you. Chaya had asked me whether you ought to go with her, and I . . ." He stopped, his head down. "I said no," he murmured huskily. "I thought it might embarrass you or make you feel pressured. Just think what could have happened if she had listened to me. What do I know?" He sounded distraught.

"Let's have that wine, Uncle Yitz," Marne said.

He straightened up, shaking himself as if he were a wet dog or a bear. He poured out the wine, raised his glass, and intoned a blessing, then smiled broadly. "*L'chaim,* and thank you, Marne."

"*L'chaim,*" Marne echoed, and she drank the wine, savoring the rich, deep taste.

Yitz said, "This never happened before. Chaya always uses that cove. What was it? What could have attacked her?"

"The doctor said it was probably an eel. He could see teeth marks."

"An eel!" Yitz exclaimed.

"A moray, unkosher eel," said Marne, half smiling.

Yitz slapped his thigh, grinning. "Ha!" he exclaimed. "Yes, unkosher, for sure." He paused and grew serious. "This never happened before," he repeated. "She must have gotten too near the rocks."

"That's what the doctor thought. A freak accident, he said."

"There are no accidents," Yitz said solemnly. "Things happen for a reason."

Marne's heart lurched. Was that really true? What could possibly be the reason for getting slashed by an eel? What could be the reason for a little girl to be kidnapped and maybe killed? When Jody vanished, nobody looked for a reason, only for a perpetrator. How could there be a reason for something so senseless?

Yitz stood up and turned to her. "You were magnificent, Marne. So strong! I only hope Becca can do as well in an emergency."

After Yitz left, Marne sat alone on the family room sofa, trying to relax, trying to sort out her thoughts. Yitz had said there are no accidents. Could that be true? Was everything, then, part of a great plan, guided and executed by God? But why would God bother with such a small thing as sending Marne to the beach with Chaya?

She gazed up at the wall, at the photograph of the Lubavitcher Rebbe, his hand slightly raised as if in blessing. *Saving a life,* she thought, *is no small thing. No, it's everything. As it is written: He who saves a single life, it is as if he had saved the entire world.* Marne had heard that sometime, amid all the sermons and all the explanations. Now it came to her with sudden force.

Marne went to the telephone, filled with the desire to call her father and tell him the news. *I saved a life tonight! I saved Chaya's life, and, you know, it is as if . . .* But Dad would get that odd cadence in his voice. He would think she was turning into a religious nut.

He answered in a muffled voice, "Hello!"

"Hey, Dad, what are you doing?"

"Eating dinner."

A second, silent conversation played beneath the surface. *I saved a life tonight, Dad. Are you proud of me?*

"What are you eating?" Marne said.

"Hot dogs and macaroni salad. And a dill pickle. So, what's new with you, baby?"

"Nothing much." *Yitz said I was magnificent. Dad, I*

don't know how I got the energy or the smarts to do it. I've never driven a van before. . . .

He chewed loudly, then said, "Well, I'm thinking of meeting your mom in Paris. For a little vacation." He paused, as if he expected her to object or maybe ask to come along.

"Sounds great," Marne said. "Let me know." *The doctor said I did exactly the right thing. How did I know what to do? I suppose I heard it somewhere, but in that moment it came together.*

"Oh, sure. I'll call you," said her dad.

The conversation drifted off into silence. "Well, I'd better go," Marne said. "It's late."

"Sleep well. Call me soon, baby."

In her bed, Marne felt the waves of tiredness, the kaleidoscope of events replaying, and that feeling of command that had propelled her to action.

"Thank You, God," Marne whispered, "for being there when I needed You."

For the next two days, Yitz supervised the day camp, and Marne was elevated to head counselor, deciding on projects and events. It was both exciting and exhausting.

220

Everyone asked her advice, even Yitz. Soon Chaya insisted on going back.

"Do you need me to be there?" Marne asked.

"No. I've got Becca and Jonathan. You need a day off," Chaya said, giving her a grateful smile. "Besides, your friend is coming today, isn't she?"

"They got in late last night," Marne said. "Kim left a message on my cell phone."

"Where is she staying?"

"At the Surf Club Condos."

"Too far for you to walk," Chaya said. "I'll drop you there."

Kim was wide awake and ready to go when Marne called. "It's so beautiful here!" she exclaimed. "Come on over. Can you spend the day?"

"Sure. I can't wait to see you," Marne said. "My aunt can drop me off."

"Great! Come for breakfast. Hey, how are you?"

"Terrific. I can't wait to see you," Marne repeated.

Chaya let her off in front of the building and sped away, the kids yelling and waving. "We'll miss you!" called Nissim and the twins. Yossi waved a scarf out the window. Marne waited for them to leave before she rang the bell. "Call me when you're ready to come home," Chaya had told her.

Suddenly there was Kim, dressed in her lime green bikini and a long, flowing beach skirt tied around her waist. Her lips shone with lip gloss, her eyes sparkled beneath green eye shadow, and she wore long, glittery earrings. "Kim!" Marne screamed.

"Marne, oh my God, it's so great to see you!" Kim shrieked. "You look great! You're so tan! I can't wait to hear all about Jeff."

"I can't wait to tell you!"

Kim's sisters came rushing out. Valerie was a senior in high school, so glamorous with her long, streaked hair and perfect manicure. Bianca, the oldest, went to junior college and worked part-time in a law firm, filing papers. Janet, the youngest, was thirteen, sweet and shy. "My little slowpoke," her father called her, squeezing her waist, and Janet would always giggle.

"Hey, Marne!" they cried, crowding around her. "Kim's been going crazy without you."

"Come on," Kim said. "My dad got us doughnuts and coffee. He got you a latte, your favorite."

"Oh, that's so sweet!" Marne exclaimed. She heard the different inflection in her voice, matching Kim's exu-

222

berance, and she felt as if she had just slipped out of a part in a play back into her own character, where she belonged.

Kim's parents were sitting on high stools at the breakfast bar, wearing terry cloth robes and slippers. Kim's mother had her hair down around her shoulders, and her face shone. She looked young and relaxed. In the background came music from an old Bette Midler album. Kim said brightly, "We all brought our favorite CDs. I got three new ones at the mall, same day I bought your flip-flops." She handed Marne a yellow plastic bag with large blue lettering, KIT AND KABOODLE.

"Oh, Kim, I love them!" Marne cried, pulling off her sandals and slipping her feet into the flip-flops. They were thick-soled and purple, with a white daisy on the top strap. "Adorable! What do I owe you?"

"It's a gift," Kim said, smiling, giving Marne a hug.

"I want you girls to go and have a good time," said Kim's father. He reached for his wallet, took out a credit card, and handed it to Valerie. "Now, you be careful with this," he said in a mock-stern voice. "I want you to guard it with your life!"

"I will, Daddy," said Valerie, giving him a quick kiss on the cheek, and her dad gave her a light, backhanded slap on the bottom.

223

"So, how's your summer so far, Marne?" he asked.

"Oh, just fine, Mr. Hadley," Marne said. She always felt a trifle awkward around Kim's parents. They didn't seem like parents, but more like two counselors halfheartedly chaperoning a field trip.

"Have a doughnut!" he urged, handing Marne the box. "I hear they don't have calories in Hawaii. Besides," he laughed heartily, "I saw this huge Hawaiian dame, biggest—"

"Hey, Jim!" his wife remonstrated, grinning.

"Sorry, Marne. They tell me I'm so crude!" He reached out and put his hand on his wife's back, lifting her hair.

"Let's go!" Valerie said. She turned to her parents. "Maybe we'll stay out all day."

"Mind if we stay out for dinner?" Bianca asked.

"No, you girls go ahead. Just take care of Janet."

"Have a good time!" chirped their mother.

"I want to go to Waikiki," Kim said.

Dimly Marne remembered that Becca had said something about making s'mores out on the beach tonight, but it probably wouldn't work out anyway. Chaya wouldn't feel up to it. "Sure, I'd love to," Marne said.

She had worn her bikini under her pink shirt and capri

pants, and she had rolled up her white gauze skirt in her bag, just in case.

"My dad rented a car," Bianca said. "So we can go where we want." She tossed up the keys and deftly caught them. "You can show us the ropes, Marne!"

Marne laughed. "What do you want to see first, the town, the stores, or the surfers?"

"Surfers!" the three of them chorused, giggling, and Janet echoed, "Surfers!"

Kim and her sisters laughed and danced around Marne. They all shared a certain look, as if they'd been polished, with their terrific teeth and wide smiles and shining hair. Beside them, Marne felt a little too short, too freckled, and she hated the way her hair got frizzy in the humidity. Kim and her sisters were so sleek.

With a quick motion Marne drew back her hair, clipped it with the silver barrette. She undid the top button of her shirt and tied the ends together, leaving her midriff bare.

"Have fun, girls!" Kim's parents called, waving from the door.

"Be good!" called their mother.

"If you can't be good, be careful!" laughed their father.

They got into the car, shrieking, and squeezed together.

"Which way, Marne?" Bianca asked.

Marne pointed. "I'll show you the beach at Waikiki. We can park and walk along hotel row. In front of the Royal Hawaiian there's a surfer school. We'll check it out. Later we can have lunch at this great hotel across the way. They have a fabulous buffet lunch and palm trees inside, in the courtyard."

The girls listened to her, absorbed and impressed.

"Now," Kim said, "tell us about Jeff. Does he have any friends?"

"College boys?" asked Bianca.

"Does he like to party?" asked Valerie.

"Are you guys going to ditch me?" asked Janet in a high, whiny voice.

"Don't worry, honey," said Kim. "Wherever we go, you can come, too. Just keep the faith," said Kim.

It sounded strange to Marne's ears. The last time she had heard that expression was when old Sol said it: "Whatever happened back then, you have to keep the faith." He had smiled at her, his face reamed with lines, especially about the eyes. He had patted her hand. "Isn't that right, Marne? We have to keep the faith."

chapter SIXTEEN

It was no coincidence. Marne knew exactly where the boys went surfing. If the waves were puny, they'd take the truck—an old red pickup that belonged to Jeff's friend Brad—and head for the other side of the island. But if the surf was decent, they liked to stay at Waikiki, where the tourists came and the *haole* girls hung around all day getting tan, wearing flowers in their hair, drinking frothy drinks that they got from the straw-roofed huts at the fancy hotels.

Of course, since Jeff had hurt his ankle, he might be at the golf club.

Marne led her friends to all the sights, the Halekulani with its high towers, the expansive Reef, the elegant Royal Hawaiian. Each hotel had its own personality. They walked through the lobbies, went into the shops, examining elaborate beach bags, sparkling sheer tops, incredibly high-heeled sandals. Music surrounded them as they sauntered through the long open-air passage with its array of merchant stalls and shops linking one grand hotel to another. They stopped for a taste of mini-tacos. Bianca bought a silver bracelet. Kim tried on shell earrings. They stopped again for frozen chocolate-covered bananas, then they made their way out to the beach. The water shone turquoise blue, as if it were lit from below, the color of jewels. The girls stood there, amazed and exuberant. Little kids splashed at the shore and chased the waves. Swimmers and surfers competed for their share of the ocean.

"Look at the crowd!" Kim cried.

"I want to go swimming," shouted Janet, tossing aside her sandals and running into the surf. She thrust herself headlong into the water, then emerged with her hair streaked down over her face, laughing rapturously. "Hey, this is the greatest."

"Look at those gorgeous guys," Valerie sighed.

"Let's find out about getting surfboards," said Bianca.

Then Marne saw Brad. He wore nose clips around his neck and a black bathing suit. His skin glistened wetly, and his hair was plastered straight down from the surf. His shoulders were enormous, his jaw firm, like a warrior or a football player. He walked past Marne, then stopped and turned back. "Marne! Hey, what's up?" With a swift glance he sized up the other girls and gave them an engaging smile.

Behind him came Jeff, hobbling a little but holding his surfboard. "Marne! How cool! This must be your friend Kim."

"Kim, this is Jeff. Jeff . . ." Marne made the introductions, feeling like a hostess, smooth and in control. It was a new feeling.

"So, what are you doing here?" Brad asked.

"We thought we'd try surfing," said Valerie, giving Brad a penetrating look. She wore a red-flowered bikini. In a flowing, elaborate gesture, she pulled back her hair, then let it fall down around her shoulders.

"Well, I guess we could show you a few things," Jeff said.

"Yeah," said Brad. "We sure could." He called out, "Hey, Chris! Come over here, pal. Want to give these girls a surfing lesson?"

Chris, blond and blue-eyed, was there in a moment, skidding down into the sand beside Kim. "Hello there," he said. "Have you done much surfing?"

"Not exactly," Kim said. She shook her head, and her earrings sparkled. "Are you a good teacher?"

"The best."

"Really? How do I know? How can I trust you?" she asked, widening her eyes and her smile.

"Want to see?"

"Yes. Show me."

Marne turned to Jeff. "Looks like your ankle is better."

"Better, but not all better," he said. "I couldn't stand another round of golf. The doctor said I can go back out on my board, if I'm not too wild."

"He looks wild to me," Valerie put in, laughing.

"Why don't you all come on and we'll take you out?" Jeff said. "I'll take Marne, and . . ."

"Valerie and Bianca," said Brad, with an arm around each of them. "We'll head out. . . . I can get you boards from my friend over there. They call him Drift. . . . He rents 'em out, usually, but he won't charge you. We'll all paddle out together, and what you do is, when you see the wave behind you, first you get up on one knee, arms out for balance, then slowly up, one foot behind the other, like this. . . ."

Chris came running back, wet and shining, presenting himself to Kim. "Satisfied?"

"You looked great," Kim purred. "I'll never be able to do that. I'm so clumsy."

"No, no," Chris said, taking her arm.

Soon it was settled, with Janet sitting on a towel watching all their stuff, and the girls paddling out, Marne with Jeff, Kim with Chris, and Brad on his board between Bianca and Valerie.

"I hope you can all swim!" Chris yelled after they had paddled out several hundred yards.

Everyone laughed. "Wouldn't you save us?"

"Ten summers of swim school!"

"I was a lifeguard at camp."

Marne's shoulders ached, and she felt nervous about the waves breaking so far from shore. She had never felt completely at ease in the ocean. What she loved best was running on the shore. But Jeff gave her a reassuring smile. "I'll be right behind you," he said.

And when she took a moderate wave and came in, catching her board on the first try, he shouted out, "Good job! Great!"

They took two or three more waves, until Jeff's ankle began to hurt, and they came in and lay on the sand.

"You're very good," Jeff said. "Not only at surfing. Very, very good."

It was the kind of fabulous day that never seems to happen to real people, Marne thought, only in stories and

231

movies or to other girls. She had never laughed so much, eaten so much, or told so many jokes and stories. She was quick and clever and funny. They ate hamburgers on the beach. They walked, holding hands, kicking up sand, laughing and chasing one another into the water. They lay in the sand, arms touching, hands clasped. When the boys went to get sodas, the girls whispered to Marne, "Where did you find these guys? They're so darling. They're all so funny. And so cute. Chris says he'll call his friend Dylan, and maybe all eight of us can go out . . . What about Janet? Don't worry, we'll take care of her. . . . She's okay. . . . Aren't they darling? This guy Dylan is a junior at the university. They said they want to take us out to dinner at a Thai place. I just love Thai food, don't you? I love Brad's physique. I love Chris's smile. Marne, you're a genius! Isn't this magic? It's paradise. Marne, those guys are so cool!"

The next few days passed in a haze of pleasure, long bottled up—no kids, no day camp, no running to clean up messes, no watching for infractions and feeling guilty about wanting a shrimp cocktail or a taco, no having to explain anything. Kim's parents were so casual, so cool. They went scuba diving. They took a sunset catamaran cruise. They played tennis with their daughters, a wild round-robin game that included Marne, seven people on one court. It was a blast. Best of all, Marne felt part of the clan, as they called themselves, the Hadley Clan. Five girls, six women! Kim's dad would roll his eyes and laugh and take a swing, as if he were hitting a golf ball. When he played golf, "the girls" went shopping in the fashionable Waikiki shops. Kim and Marne bought fake designer purses, delighted by their purchase.

"Now, you come on and bring those boyfriends of yours over for barbecue one night, you hear?" said Kim's mom. Marne loved her Southern drawl and the easy manner that went with it. "We'll just put up some steaks and baked potatoes; boys love steaks. I saw a nice bakery where we can get coconut cream pies. You tell them all to come on; we'll have us a great ole time!"

Kim invited Marne to sleep over at their condo for the weekend. "The boys want to take us to the beach Saturday night; they've got everything planned, isn't that adorable?"

Marne shook her head. "I'll have to ask my aunt."

"So? Ask her. Why wouldn't she let you come?"

"You don't understand. She's . . . different. Her kids always stay home."

"Well, we're almost family, aren't we? You're part of the clan! Tell her that."

"Friday night . . ." Marne bit her lip. How to explain the process, the utterly consuming experience that was *Shabbos*? She couldn't compare it to a birthday or to Christmas; they came only once a year. And Kim would object: "What's the big deal? It happens every week, doesn't it? So, why can't you miss one time?" And Marne would get that strange uncomfortable feeling, being so different, being so weird.

It was like that when Jody disappeared. Her mom insisted that she go to the camp reunion, wanting her to "get back into the swing of things." Marne didn't want to go, but it wasn't worth protesting. At the reunion everyone looked at her as if she had blue skin or something. Nobody spoke. They only stared at Marne, looking embarrassed. The camp director gave her a huge card that everyone had signed. And Marne thanked her, but she couldn't stand to look at the card or to show it to Mom. She tore it up into many, many pieces and slowly flushed it down the toilet.

She told Mom about the card later, half afraid, but her mother wasn't mad. She just held out her arms and

234

gathered Marne very close, and the two of them stayed that way for a long time.

"I'll call my mom," Marne told Kim. "She'll say it's fine, and then my aunt won't have anything to complain about."

"Your aunt sounds like a witch," Kim muttered.

"She's just nervous."

"I guess."

Marne calculated the time in Paris. Early morning meant it was evening there. Marne called at seven, even before she went out for her run.

"Darling!" Her mother's voice was filled with pleasure. "How wonderful to hear from you tonight. I had the most marvelous day. A group of us went to the Palace of Versailles, and it is gorgeous. Absolutely gorgeous. How *are* you? Did Kim come yet?"

"Yes. And we're having a marvelous time. Marvelous."

"That's wonderful. How are her parents?"

"They invited me to spend the weekend. They're in this gorgeous condo right on the beach, with a huge pool. It's so much fun, Mom! Is it okay if I spend the weekend with them?"

"Of course. Why not?"

"Well, would you tell your sister? Chaya?"

"Oh, I get it." There was an odd silence. "Sure. Put her on."

Friday night they went to the movies, nine of them. Kim had put up a mild protest, whining a little. "Do we have to take Janet? She's such a baby!"

Her father had spoken sternly. "You know the rules, Kimmy. You girls stick together when you're away from home."

"There's safety in numbers, sweetie," Kim's mom explained in her pleasant drawl. "Now, you all take care Janet doesn't get into any trouble." Marne listened with fascination at the way she dropped the *s* in *doesn't*. It sounded so cool. *Dunnt*.

Janet kept whispering during the movie, until Valerie bought her a double-huge carton of buttered popcorn. Saturday was another glorious day at Waikiki, swimming, paddleboarding, hanging out, and laughing a lot. And Marne, imagining the dingy hotel with its torn chairs and Coke machine, felt almost giddy at being out on the beach amid the crowd, with all the noise and the laughter, the music and the pounding surf.

After a long day at the beach they all went back to Kim's condo and showered and did their hair, and Mr. Hadley yelped, "It's like a goddamn beauty parlor in here!" But he sounded more pleased than annoyed, and when they were all dressed again to go out, he stood at the door grinning. "I've got me a bevy of beauties here!"

Now Janet was stuffing a bunch of magazines into her backpack while Bianca and Valerie packed up the car with blankets and sweatshirts, in case of rain.

Kim gathered a handful of CDs. "Janet's crazy about these," she murmured to Marne. "Keeps her engrossed for hours."

Marne nodded. She noticed that Kim's words also bore a trace of an Alabama accent; somehow she hadn't noticed that before.

"The guys said they'll meet us at the surfer hut at around six," Kim said. "They know this private beach where we can cook out and swim."

Bianca and Valerie stood at the window, whispering together. Valerie pulled something out of her bag, held it in her palm for a moment, then shoved it back.

"Kimmy!" their mom called. "You girls be sure and take those towels! You can't rely on boys to think of things like that."

Bianca, laughing, called back, "Don't worry, Mom. We've got everything we'll need."

Mrs. Hadley's voice rang in Marne's ears as they drove away in the rented car. "Now y'all have a good time!"

"Back here at midnight, no exceptions!" barked out their father.

"Yes, sir!" the sisters chorused, as if they had rehearsed it, even Janet joining in, giggling.

They drove to Waikiki, where they parked the car. Bianca locked the doors and tried them several times. "We better make sure they get us back here by quarter to twelve," she said firmly. "You know how Daddy gets."

"We won't be late," Valerie assured her. "I've got a little alarm on my cell phone."

"Really?" Bianca exclaimed, giving her sister a poke. "You clever old thing!"

"Marne," Valerie said, "Brad is so cool. He said he's coming to California this fall to start college. I had no idea you'd be collecting so many cool guys."

"All in just a few weeks," Kim added with a proud smile. "Chris is taking me out kayaking tomorrow morning at the other side of the island."

"Cool," said Marne.

They met the boys by Brad's truck. Chris's college friend, Dylan, agreed to drive. He looked very serious with his close-cropped hair, rimless glasses, and wiry body. But he was high-energy, used to taking charge. "You guys get in the back," he said. "Me and my old lady don't like crowds." He laughed, and Bianca puckered her lips and blew him a kiss. They climbed into the cab, while Marne and the others got into the back, sitting on folded blankets. Marne had never ridden in the back of a truck before. She loved the feel of the wind in her hair and Jeff's leg brushing hers.

They drove beyond the hotels, down to the highway, past the strip mall, where just a few days ago Marne had taken Chaya. She remembered her feelings of panic, the way she took charge, and how Chaya and Yitz had praised her. It felt so good not to have to be in charge of anything now, just to be sitting in the truck bed with Jeff clasping her hand in his. Across from them, Kim and Chris were snuggled together, and Valerie and Brad were kissing, a succession of swift, funny little kisses, followed by laughter and then a real kiss.

Dylan slowed the truck and put his head out the window to yell, "Want to stop here? It's nice." Bianca turned around and waved at them through the rear window.

Marne got up on her knees. "Not a good spot," she said.

"What do you mean?" Jeff asked, standing up.

"Eels hide out by those rocks. We shouldn't swim there."

Jeff, looking impressed, relayed the message to Dylan. "Go up about another mile or two," he shouted. "There's a real neat beach with good sand and no rocks or coral."

"You've got it!" Dylan shouted back. The truck lurched forward so suddenly that Marne and Jeff slid down, she on top of him, and then his arms were around her, tight.

Above them the sky was beginning to offer its brilliant panorama. The horizon glowed crimson and gold, then deep purple. The brilliant sunset, the gentle sweet breeze, and Jeff all provided the perfect paradise she had hoped for.

chapter SEVENTEEN

The boys had brought boxes full of food—potato chips and hot dogs, marshmallows, a huge bag of chocolate chip cookies, and a pineapple, already cut into fat round slices neatly fitted into a plastic bag and tied with a twist. Brad carried the largest bag, filled with drinks.

"Did you have any trouble getting the beer?" Chris asked Brad.

"Dylan got it. They always card me."

"Me too."

"Got anything stronger?"

"Some liquor my dad keeps way back in the bar. They'll never miss it."

"Or they'll think the maid stole it," Chris said, laughing. His arm was around Kim's waist.

"That's so mean!" Kim objected in a drawling, childish voice. "Don't you even care if the maid loses her job, all because of you?" She sounded petulant, but she was grinning up at Chris.

241

He gave her a hug. "Come on. Let's start a fire." He popped open several cans of beer and distributed them.

Marne held the can in her hands, the coldness a welcome touch. She took a sip and quickly swallowed. She had never cared for the taste. Her dad said it was something you develop, and she had argued, "Why would you want to develop it if it tastes awful?" And he had grinned and put his arm around her. "That's my girl—I guess I don't have to worry about you."

Of course, he did worry. Her dad was so funny. He brought home circulars with the innocuous letters NIDA sprinkled across the top, and he left them casually on the kitchen counter or the coffee table. He didn't act like an enforcer or sit her down for a conversation about how he trusted her and all that garbage, designed to conceal the fact that this discussion was all about drugs and drinking. He had told her about having made "a couple of stupid mistakes" during his college days, how he felt like a jerk now even thinking about it. No pressure; he never asked her for any promises. But he got that look on his face, sort of a smile and worry blended together, and then he put his hand on the top of her head, his way of saying "I love you."

Chris squashed his empty beer can and opened another. He offered one to Marne. She shook her head. "I'm still working on this one," she said lightly, taking several more swallows. Dad was right. It didn't taste so bad now.

Brad motioned the boys into a huddle. They stood there looking oddly serious. Dylan reached into his pocket and distributed something to the others. Craig took some bills from his wallet and gave them to Dylan.

Kim laughed and pointed. "Aren't they so cute? What do you think they're talking about?"

"Us!" Valerie squealed, laughing, and Bianca giggled in a strange way, shimmying her body from side to side, as if she was dancing on the stage. Their attitude, their expressions were different tonight. All week they'd gone surfing and hiking and sat on the beach solving sudoku puzzles that Dylan brought. They laughed a lot and told jokes; nobody seemed to take anything too seriously. Tonight felt different.

Marne glanced at Bianca. She smiled, envying Bianca's gorgeous blond hair, just as she envied Bianca's composure and confidence. "I wish I had your hair," she murmured.

"No, you don't," Bianca said. "It's a pain to keep this

243

up. You, on the other hand," she said with a wide smile, "are a natural redhead. That's really something."

Jeff came to take Marne's hand. "Come on, gorgeous," he said. "Let's eat." They sat down on the sand. Brad had brought a CD player, turned on full volume, so that it felt like a rock concert out under the stars, a concert in paradise, everything perfect.

The hot dogs were crisp and delicious. Even the mustard, plain old yellow mustard, tasted terrific. "Mustard," Jeff said, pointing, "at the edge of your mouth." He bent his head. He wiped it away with the tip of his tongue. "Mmmm. Good."

Marne settled back, feeling relaxed now, letting the sound of the waves soothe her. This was good. This was what she had dreamed of. She belonged. And she had, in a way, created all this by meeting Jeff and getting everyone together. It was the perfect beach party. They ate all the marshmallows, plain, agreeing after much discussion and laughter that nobody liked them roasted, anyhow.

"Want another beer?" Jeff asked.

"I don't really like it," Marne said. "First time I ever drank a whole one."

"Try this—tastes like candy." He poured a colorless,

thick liquid into a paper cup, took a sip, and handed it to her.

Marne held the liquid in her mouth for a moment, then let it slide down her throat, thick and sweet and oddly familiar. "It's like licorice," she said. "Actually, it's delicious."

"Goes down easy," Jeff said, leaning back, looking older, sophisticated.

Bianca and Dylan were locked in conversation punctuated with laughter. They got up to dance, their movements sharp and mechanical, like something out of a movie. Marne looked down at her cup. Somehow it had gotten filled again. She sipped slowly, savoring the taste, feeling the slight tingle now, thinking, *I'm buzzed*. She said the words aloud, ending with a giggle. Jeff gave her a quick squeeze. He bent to kiss her. She tasted the sweetness on his lips, on the tip of his tongue.

The music seemed to swallow the air around them, louder than the waves.

Bianca, swishing her beach skirt around her hips, fluttered her hands, drawing them close. "You guys," she said in a husky tone, "remember we've got to be home at midnight. And you all have to stay cool. Hear?"

Valerie licked her lips. "We're cool. Don't worry." She glanced at Kim.

"I'm cool." Kim giggled.

"Dylan got these here," Bianca said. She opened her hand. On her palm lay half a dozen small tablets.

"What is it?" Marne asked.

"Candy," Valerie said. "Happy candy."

"Well, I don't know." Marne felt her heart pound. "It's just . . . my dad says pills can be . . . ."

"These aren't dangerous," Bianca said. She gazed at Marne, her blue eyes very deep and earnest. "Do you think I'd give you anything that was harmful?" She looked hurt, her eyes moist. "But of course, nobody's telling you . . . ."

Kim said, "Nobody's forcing you, Marne."

"It's just that I never . . . ," Marne whispered.

Valerie looked troubled. "Look, we didn't realize that you'd freak out."

Kim gave her a slight push. "She's not freakin' out, Val! Leave her alone. Marne's just bein' a good little girl." They giggled.

It was hard to tell exactly when things started slipping away from Marne. At first it was like looking into a mirror that had just developed a thin crack. Something was off, just a little. But the crack deepened and widened, until nothing seemed solid or normal anymore. Somehow Kim had gotten Janet back into the truck, along with the whole bag of chocolate chip cookies. "Just relax in the car, honey," Kim drawled. "You can lay back and hear the music. I brought all your favorite CDs, and Brad's going to play 'em for you, isn't that nice?" Marne noticed, in a strange, dreamlike way, that Kim had dropped the *s* from *isn't,* and it came out like *in'it.*

"Now you be sure and say thank you to Brad. We're going to go down there by the water. It's gettin' cold now. It might even rain. Dylan said so. You just stay here nice and dry and listen to the music and eat those cookies, only don't eat 'em all, you hear?"

Kim's voice and manner were entirely new to Marne. She mirrored her sisters, became different, transplanted here to an island where there were no rules and no limits. It was as if the world had exploded into sound and motion and crazy patterns of light and shadow, scenes shifting like a music video. Kim and Chris, Brad and Valerie, Bianca and Dylan were all dancing, bumping into each other, changing partners, dancing solo, shouting, "Yeah! Yeah! All right!" Sweat layered their faces. Dylan's hair was wet with it. His arms pumped wildly, his body gyrated. He caught Bianca in his arms, swung her up, dropped her down, and the two of them lay on the sand, screaming with laughter.

"Sorry I can't dance," Jeff said loudly, close to Marne's ear. "My ankle . . ."

It seemed as if there were many more people here, not just Kim and her sisters, for the laughter and shouts and music rang in Marne's ears like feedback from a microphone. She sat down on the sand beside Jeff, and he kissed her while the music played and played. Then she was lying down close beside him on the blanket, and Jeff's hands moved over her body while in the distance words seemed to float around her, *What's going on? What's going on?*

Kim and Chris sat under a banyan tree, their faces turned to the sky, their expressions frozen, rapt. Marne saw them get up to dance again, their hands clenched into fists, as if they were enraged. They danced faster and faster, their bodies grinding, faces gleaming.

And Marne remembered a conversation with Kim. It seemed long ago. "Bianca's kinda wild," she had said. "She gets herself into all kinds of stuff, and Daddy thinks she's such a little angel."

"What kind of stuff?" Marne had prompted.

"You name it," Kim replied. "Mostly club stuff. Sometimes she gets crazy. But she knows when to stop."

Crazy. They were all crazy. And Marne, watching, felt as if she were sitting at the edge of the planet, looking down, afraid she might fall.

Now Jeff was moving closer, his body on hers, his weight holding her down.

"Jeff," she gasped, "I need to . . ."

"Marne, Marne," he moaned. "Oh, Marne . . . wait. I have to get something."

Marne lay in the sand, watching Jeff run to Dylan, his shape wavering, and she sat up and took a deep breath. A bottle of water lay nearby. She reached for it and drank deeply. From some other, distant place came a voice, demanding her attention. *What are you doing? What are you doing?* Marne stood up. She felt odd, hot and cool at the same time.

Dylan and Bianca, their bodies two shadowy mounds blended together on a blanket, started when Jeff approached. "What the hell's the matter with you?" Dylan bellowed. His arm swung out at Jeff. "Stupid kid, take care of your own . . ."

The two of them argued. Jeff shouted, "You're such a nerd!"

Marne saw Chris going to the cooler for more beer, and Kim was beside Marne, kneeling in the sand. The music was suddenly off; the silence seemed eerie. "Marne, are you okay?" Kim's face above her showed concern. "Listen, honey, you don't have to do anything. . . . I mean, just make Jeff feel good. You know what I mean? We talked about it. Just make him feel good. He's such a sweet guy. Don't you like him?"

Now Jeff knelt beside Marne, smiling down at her. "Don't you like me?"

Slowly Marne felt her sensations returning. "Yes," she whispered. "Yes, I like you. But . . ."

"Well. Come on. Relax."

She lay down again, grateful for the firm sand beneath her, for the spinning of her head at last slowing down. At the edge of things, Marne heard the others. They were all singing and laughing. They were cool. Bianca knew what she was doing. She knew when to stop. Bianca wouldn't let anything bad happen to them. And Marne was with them, part of the clan, the Hadley Clan.

"Marne, Marne," Jeff murmured. Now it was Tris and the Triplets singing a love song, Marne's favorite, and she wanted to listen to the words, but other words intruded. *What are you doing? It's not for you. Not for you. You're a person. Your own person.* The voices blended—Chaya's, her father's, her own. *What are you doing?*

She pulled away from Jeff so suddenly that her elbow struck his chin. He flinched, hand to his mouth, and rolled flat onto his back. "Hey! What's wrong?"

Marne looked down at his sprawled figure, his bare chest with the medal on the leather cord, that medal she had thought looked so good. He gazed up at her, perplexed, frankly troubled. "What's wrong, Marne? Did I do something . . . I thought you liked me. . . ."

She stood there for a moment, about to explain: *Yes, I do like you. It's not your fault. It's me. Maybe I'm weird. Maybe I'm from Mars; something must be wrong with me, but I can't. . . . It's not for me. I'm a person. A person.*

"I have to go," Marne gasped. She scooped up her sandals, her bag, tucked them under her arms.

"Go where?" Jeff yelped, bewildered. He got up, reaching toward her. "Where would you go? Listen, I . . . What's wrong with you? Dylan," he called, as if he were seeking reinforcements, someone to help him out. But Dylan did not respond. He and Bianca were lost from view, lost in the music that still crashed around them, obliterating voices, even obliterating the sound of the waves.

Marne took several deep breaths. She steadied herself. The liquor left her mouth dry, and her head still felt light. But the acute dizziness was past. She knew exactly where she was going and how long it would take. Along that dark road, running on the sandy shoulder, it would take her nearly an hour, but that was okay. She was a good runner.

Time seemed to be warped. She had heard of time warp in space travel and in science fiction, when the ordinary became strange and unpredictable. Just so was this road, her own breathing loud against the serene night, her feet on the thin layer of sand making swishing sounds. Soon she caught the rhythm, focused on the distant stars and on the motions of her body, all thoughts emptying away. Only this, the night and her movements, was real and meaningful. Later she would think. Later she would argue with herself back and forth. She would cry. But now, all she knew was that she had to move forward.

Headlights blazed a broken path in front of her; the car pulled up alongside. Jeff leaned out, calling, "Marne! What the hell is the matter with you? Have you gone nuts?"

His voice was shrill and broken. "Where are you going? What are you going to do?"

Marne glanced over without breaking her stride.

Dylan's face was turned straight ahead. He looked furious, his jaw set, mouth compressed.

Jeff called again. "Marne, if you want to go home, at least let us drive you."

Marne kept on running, counting her steps . . . ten, twelve, fourteen.

The boys conferred, muttering. Dylan's hands struck the steering wheel in anger. Jeff called again. "What are you going to tell your aunt? We didn't do anything. We didn't do anything to you."

"Go away!" Marne shouted.

"You're crazy," Jeff offered. The truck rolled slowly along beside her. "Come on, Marne. Get in. This is ridiculous."

Marne kept on running, her mind focused on the feel of her feet now hitting the pavement.

At last Dylan swung the truck around and Marne heard him grumbling, "Let her go, Jeff. She's a nutcase. We were having a good time. . . ."

Marne heard the truck's engine waning as it moved

away, and she sped ahead, running faster and faster, until she felt the endorphins kick in. It was a long run, longer than any she had ever attempted. And as she ran, things occurred to her, ideas exploded through her mind like fireworks. The night seemed to mark the end of something, or a beginning.

The house was oddly silent when Marne got there. A light was on in the kitchen; otherwise it was dark. Her feet were blistered and sore, and she was achingly tired, but highly alert.

In the bathroom, she took a towel from the drawer, saturated it with cold water, and sat on the edge of the tub wiping her feet. The bathroom was cluttered with toys, as usual, but somehow it didn't matter. The odors of wet towels and soap and the bubble bath Esti used all converged and brought Marne back to the days before Kim and her family came, the days she had counted off and now wished she could simply cancel.

A cool shower took away her tiredness. Quickly Marne dried herself, then dressed in her capri pants and striped shirt. Through the bedroom window Marne heard distant laughter and a song. It was Jonathan's voice, strong and spirited, singing in Hebrew.

Marne stepped outside, past the small yard and to the beach. They were all gathered around a fire, the kids roasting things on long sticks. Yitz, his body a tall, dark shadow, moved from one to the other. Laughter rang out. Chaya clapped in rhythm to the singing.

Marne ran back to get her guitar. With it she hurried out, calling as she went, "Hey! Looks like you guys are having a beach party! I guess you need some music."

They all turned to her, their faces bright in the fire-light, their voices clear and welcoming.

"We're having s'mores!" Esti shouted.

Becca came toward her, holding out a toasted marsh-mallow and a graham cracker. "Are you mad we didn't wait for you? We didn't know you'd be home."

"Sit, sit!" called Chaya, still clapping to the rhythm of Jonathan's tune.

Marne sank down in the sand and bent over her gui-tar. It felt good in her arms, and the warmth of the fire felt good against her skin. She looked around at the kids with their smiles and their gooey faces. "Hey, Marne!" Chaya called. "I thought you were sleeping over at your friend's tonight."

"She missed us," Yitz shouted with a grin. "Glad to see you, Marne!"

"Glad to see you, too," Marne said.

Jonathan continued to sing, as if nothing had changed. Almost by instinct, Marne picked up the tune, embellishing it with a string of broken chords, arpeggios. Jonathan sang on, his voice soaring to her accompaniment, his face turned up to the stars.

Marne heard their voices through the walls. Becca was sound asleep, she who claimed to have trouble sleeping! In her sleep she grunted softly, murmured, and Marne wondered what her little cousin dreamed about. Chaya's and Yitz's voices made a rhythmic rumble, soft but compelling. Marne felt connected to the voices, almost as if she possessed some mystical ability to hear sounds that were locked between walls.

". . . obviously a problem."

"Will you ask her about it?"

"Not unless she brings it up . . . matter of trust . . ."

"Never can tell . . . teenagers . . . Those boys . . . Do you think . . . ?"

"I think . . . scared, maybe . . . but okay . . . strong."

Trust. They trusted her. Chaya thought she was strong. Marne felt elated. She had done something right.

More than right; she had asserted herself. Shown courage, moral courage.

But another voice scorned the triumph. *What was Kim thinking? What will she say? That I'm from Mars?*

The truth was, she didn't have that many friends. There was Kim, always there, reliable, never asking any awkward questions, ready to break out and have fun. Kim would be furious at her for spoiling the party, upsetting Bianca and Valerie. Prude, they'd call her.

Marne's heart fluttered, and her chest felt heavy with anxiety. More words seemed to melt through the walls, the sounds enveloping her.

". . . teach Jonathan . . . very musical . . . He loves the guitar."

"Would he . . . his cousin . . . girls . . ."

"He asked me if he could . . ."

"What did you say?"

"I said yes."

All at once the worry was gone, replaced by this new possibility, the idea that Jonathan wanted to learn guitar and she would teach him.

"Bashert," Marne heard her aunt say, that word meaning that something was destined, preordained. There is a

reason, Yitz always said, why a Jew finds himself in a particular place. It isn't just coincidence.

Marne turned on the small bedside light on its skinny metal pole. She reached for the book, picked it up, and sat gazing at the cover. The book with its fairy-tale pictures had given her a strange comfort—why? Because it had seemed to her, in her innocence, in her grief, that somehow its pages contained a clue to the answer she so desperately needed. Why had the goblins stolen Jody away? How could such a thing happen to an innocent child?

Marne slipped the book back into her suitcase. She switched off the light and lay in the darkness. Quietly she held a conversation, a continuation of the conversation she had begun out there in the darkness, on the road.

God, I know I'll never find the reason for it. Maybe, like an earthquake or a flood, things happen because they are built into the way the world works. I don't know. Maybe finding a reason isn't the point. Maybe the point is figuring out how to move on and how to talk to You about it.

"It isn't fair," Marne said, an audible whisper.

And somehow she caught a firm reply. "You're right. It isn't."

chapter EIGHTEEN

It was not just an ordinary run. The night, the utter darkness of sky broken only by sharp stars, the smell of salt and sand, the fear of stumbling and falling, of being struck from behind, of a sudden cramp rendering her helpless—all these thoughts lay upon Marne as she began to run. Behind her, Jeff and Kim and Chris were calling her name in that oddly expectant, half-anxious and half-teasing tone, suggesting that she would surely recover her senses and come back. But Marne ran on. Even after Jeff and Dylan got into the truck, pulled up alongside her, sending great swatches of light all around her, she did not relent. In her mind nothing mattered except the rhythm and the pace—forward movement, legs reaching, feet touching, springing, stretching, arms pacing, heart pumping, over and over and over again.

The truck swung around and vanished. And then there was nothing but the sky and the sandy road and the sound of the roaring waves matching the persistent pulsing

259

in her throat. If it took forever, she vaguely thought, she would continue. She wished it were a twenty-mile run or more. She needed time to tune her mind to her body, to let go of everything that had happened on the beach—the laughter, the frantic dancing, the groping, the drugs, the desire, and the aversion. All of it seemed to hang on her like a weight that would fall from her back only if she ran long enough and hard enough. And so she ran.

And as Marne ran, patterns formed in her mind, rotating, repeating: *What was I thinking? What was I thinking? What was I thinking? Notnotnotnotnot.*

Her pulse climbed and her breath came in great gulps, then smoothed out into the runner's even tempo. And after a time—was it a long, long time?—as she moved into that measured pace, Marne understood how close she had come to that state where thought no longer mattered, reason no longer mattered. She had been on the brink of non-reason, non-feeling, non-pain. And she knew full well that she had not been deceived. She had not been swept away. No. Part of her had ridden the wave, as a surfer does, wanting to be caught and lifted, wanting to be pushed along. She had wanted to escape to the place where she no longer needed to question or to grieve.

But she had stood up. She had left. And she was running home, like a child—or like a person. The word *person* became a signpost in Marne's mind, and she recalled all the times Chaya had used it as praise or as a reprimand. *Be a person!* And interwoven with that admonition came Yitz's voice reciting his favorite psalm: *"Do not put your trust in mortal man."* She had, by now, attended over a dozen of Yitz's services, and always he led the people in that psalm and gave a brief commentary on it; a *drash,* he called it. *"Do not put your trust in mortal man; rely on God. Only upon God."*

But God is distant. He is inscrutable. Even when we seek Him, how is He to be found? And when we find Him, why doesn't He answer? Round and round, like a hopeless wheel of fortune that never lands on the prize, the questions continued, posed by Yitz himself, argued by the listeners or in the long, silent thoughts that came to smother a person in the middle of the night.

Now, as Marne ran and ran, pushing through the darkness, she also felt as if she was pushing through the layers of questions, the layers of doubt and struggle. Only one question remained. How do we live in this world, knowing there is evil?

As Marne ran, tears formed and spilled down her cheeks, terrible, long-repressed tears for Jody.

Where is Jody? Is she dead or alive? Why can't we find out? Oh, God, help me!

I will lift up my eyes unto the hills . . .

Jody!

I will lift up my eyes . . .

Jody! Jody!

Be a person. Be a person.

Oh, Jody . . .

Be a person.

At last her breathing, as she ran, ascended to tranquillity. Long strides, the patient beating of her heart, the renewing breath and constant nourishing oxygen flowing through her body gave Marne a sense of quiet resignation. *It is what it is. Am I going to let it spoil the rest of my life? I still have to be a person. That's what I know for sure. Maybe that is enough.*

It was ludicrous, the way Chaya kept a watchful eye out whenever Marne and Jonathan were together. *As if,* Marne thought in disgust, *she thinks I'm going to seduce him, my own cousin! A thin, pale, arrogant boy who happens to be my cousin, who happens to sing like an angel, which is the only reason I am sitting there teaching him chords. I like to hear him sing.*

It was actually more than that. Jonathan's singing lifted her up like some kind of magic or a sudden amazing physical phenomenon, like seeing the aurora borealis or an eclipse or a Hawaiian sunset.

"You're amazing," Marne told Jonathan. He had mastered six chords, and he played them like a professional, no longer bothering to look as he firmed his fingertips on the strings. He played with his head slightly thrown back, giving power to his voice, and once he began, there was almost no stopping him.

"Thanks," Jonathan said. He would not look directly at her but gave only an oblique glance.

"Lovely, Jonathan!" Chaya called, standing in the doorway.

Marne laughed to herself: *Don't worry, Chaya. I'm not corrupting your precious son.* "Are you going to get a guitar?" she asked Jonathan.

He nodded. "I'll use my *bar mitzvah* money."

"Is that okay? With your dad?"

Jonathan paused, his fingers resting lightly on the strings. "It's my money. And I'll use it for *kiddush Hashem.*"

Marne bit her lip. Not that again. "How?" she asked,

making her tone patient. They were sitting on decrepit wicker chairs on the patio out back, with the ocean surging just beyond.

Jonathan said, "When I go places, I'll use my guitar and my singing to teach people about *Hashem*. About *Shabbos*. People say I have a gift. . . ."

"You do," Marne said firmly. "The way you learn so fast, how you feel the music . . ."

"God gave me the gift. Now, I have to give it back."

"I see."

"It's like you," Jonathan said. He was perspiring; his forehead shone with sweat. He lifted his eyes, so that they were at a level with Marne's, but still they were downcast, and his gaze was totally without challenge. "You have a gift, too," Jonathan said. His tone was soft but intense. "You're—brave. You can do things that I . . . You run so many miles. You make new friends. And you teach. The little kids think you hung the moon."

"What little kids?"

"The day campers. All day long they talk about you. 'Marne said this, taught us this, Marne's so funny, we love her songs, she's so nice, she's our best friend.' "

Jonathan lifted his eyes, and he met her gaze fully.

"Do you have any idea how many of those little girls say you are their best friend?"

"Best friend," Marne murmured. She smiled. "I didn't know that."

"Well," said Jonathan, looking away, "now you know."

Little Stephanie clung to Marne's hand. "Will you help me with my sand castle?"

"Sure," Marne said. "Let's make some turrets. We can use that seaweed for a flag."

"What's a turret?"

"I don't know," Marne said, laughing. "Something with a pointy top. Like my head."

"You don't have a pointed head!" The little girl giggled and gave Marne a hug. "You're so funny, Marne! And you make the best sand castles."

As she spent more time with the children, Marne came to know their ways, their tantrums and their giggles, their fears and their delights. Five-year-old Monte loved to tell jokes. Stephanie was always laughing. Wendy wouldn't eat anything with spices in it. David rejected anything wobbly or green on his plate. More than that, they told her secrets. "My mommy's having a baby," or

"Our cat did poop on the kitchen table!" They showed her their "boo-boos," told of their daily triumphs and tragedies. "Mom got soap in my eyes when she washed my hair!" or "I went down the big waterslide by myself!"

In return, Marne gave them some secrets of her own, silly secrets that the kids, nevertheless, thought were special. "Look, I cut my leg shaving. Hey, did you know I can curl my tongue? Does your thumb bend back like this? Once I fell out of a tree and broke my wrist. It hurt so much! Let's race to that boulder. Hey—do you wanna hear a joke? There was this old bear . . ."

Suddenly she was ten again, having skipped a lot of years in between, years that were filled with trying to pretend that things were normal. Three of the day campers were girls between the ages of ten and twelve. Junior counselors, like Becca, they devised games and crafts and helped with the younger kids. And they turned to Marne more and more, asking her opinion, her help, begging her to teach them another song.

One day, quite on impulse, Marne decided to bring several books for story time. Among them was her own copy of *Outside Over There*. As she took it from her backpack, Marne felt her heart plunge in her chest, and she almost put it away again. But resolutely she gathered the children around her on their beach towels, and she held up the book.

"This," she said, "is one of my favorite stories. It's a little scary," she said, her heart pounding, "but it all turns out fine."

She read the story, showing them the pictures one by one, rotating the book so that everyone could see. The children sat quietly, eyes wide, fingers in their noses or mouths or in their hair.

"Now," Marne said when the story was told. "What do you think happened to the baby? Where did she go?"

"To the fairies," said a little girl, Abigail.

"Why did she go?" asked Marne.

"They took her," Stephanie replied.

"Why would they?" Marne asked.

The children shrugged, looked at their hands, rubbed their faces. "Don't know."

"Nobody knows," Marne finally said.

Abigail waved her hand frantically. "But God knows!" she shrieked.

"Yes," said Marne. "He does."

"Then why doesn't He tell us?" said Stephanie, pouting.

Marne felt Chaya's presence behind her. She waited for Chaya to speak. At last Marne said, "I guess if God talked to us, and we could see Him right here, we'd *have* to be good all the time. We wouldn't really be able to decide things on our own."

"Free choice," Chaya whispered at Marne's back, "has its price."

"In the story," said Stephanie, "she got the baby back."

"Yes," Marne agreed. "In the story."

Five little bodies pressed close to Marne that afternoon as they said good-bye, giving hugs and wet kisses, looking up at her adoringly. "Will you be here tomorrow?" they urged, tugging at her hands. "Will you tell us more stories? Sing more songs? Build castles?"

"Yes, yes," Marne replied to all of them.

From their car windows they waved their good-byes, yelling, "I love you, Marne!"

And Marne waved back and called, "I love you!"

She realized she had never said that to any other child but Jody.

A dozen times Marne picked up the phone to call Kim, then she laid it down again. What on earth could she say? What would Kim say? She didn't want to argue or to explain;

she didn't want to hear Kim's rationalizations. Explanations were Kim's specialty. She always got her way.

But things were unresolved. What about that night? What had happened? Was Kim still seeing Chris? Were they all going out together, having parties, roaring around the island in that old red truck?

After eight days Marne called. Mrs. Hadley answered. The sound of her voice brought a prickling sensation reaching down Marne's back. Too sugary, too attentive and kindly, Mrs. Hadley said, "Why, Marne, I was just telling Kimmy how much we miss you around here! Hope everything's all right and you're not taken sick, are you? But I guess you're busy helping your aunt with all those kids. We were hopin' you'd come and join us for the weekend, weren't we, girls?" The sisters were obviously poised around their mother, listening, holding their breath.

"Why, they're just wild to see you, hon. Honestly, we're just leaving to go to the perfume factory. Kimmy's dyin' to talk to you, but her daddy's already out in the car, and you know how he gets. She'll call you tomorrow, okay? Okay? You have a good one, darlin'!"

And Marne knew Kim wasn't going to call. She'd have given her mom some glib story. Marne could just see the way Kim tossed her hair over her shoulder, stopping as she ran from one room to another, answering her mother's airy question, "Why haven't we seen Marne around lately?"

"Oh, she's just gotten kinda weird, you know? Maybe it's from living with those weird relatives of hers. She just isn't any fun anymore, you know?"

And Mrs. Hadley would say, "Yeah, well, people change, Kimmy. It's really great you understanding that without getting bent out of shape about it."

When they got back home, things would change between her and Kim. They'd still be friends, say hello, maybe even do things together, but it wouldn't be the same. Because, even though Kim had defended her about the drugs, there was this shift. Over and over again Marne remembered the scene, with Kim telling her, "Just make Jeff feel good. Make him feel good." And Marne realized that she and Kim were on different wavelengths.

Face it, Marne told herself. *You're not part of the Hadley Clan.*

Marne thought about the girls she'd lost touch with ever since Jody disappeared. She had avoided them, unable to accept their sympathy, just like she'd torn up that card from the campers. Now, somehow she'd make

270

amends, make them her friends. . . . Marne smiled to herself. It sounded like the words to a song.

Meanwhile, Marne stopped jogging toward the surfing beach and changed her course, going north on that strip of sand bordering the highway, the same path she had taken that night. The road she chose hosted a variety of early-morning joggers. Three elderly men made their slow pace together. A couple of teenage girls in black leotards ran in tandem. Several couples made this their daily brisk walk. In a matter of days Marne recognized them all, and they seemed to accept her, calling out the Hawaiian greeting, "Aloha!"

Would they miss her, she wondered, if suddenly she was gone?

The telephone rang midmorning. Chaya was loading the kids into the van.

"Get that, Marne, would you?" she called.

"Kessler residence," Marne said.

"Hi," he said, his voice cracking slightly.

Her heart pounded.

"Don't hang up, please!"

"I—what do you want?"

"I want to see you," Jeff said. "Please."

chapter NINETEEN

They met on the pier past the surfing beach, in front of the small stand that sold soda, snacks, and sunscreen. Jeff bought two Cokes, fumbling in the pocket of his shorts for the money. He took a long time picking up the drinks, wiping them off, walking with them down to the water. For a few minutes they stood watching the waves curl onto the shore.

"Thanks for meeting me," he finally said.

Marne sat down on the sand. Jeff sat down beside her. "Have you been surfing?" she asked. She did not meet his eyes.

"No."

"Your ankle bothering you?"

"No. It's better."

Marne remained silent, looking out at the sea, as if she would memorize the pale turquoise water, serene and luminescent, until it met the darker blue beyond. For a moment she contemplated that deep ocean, where undersea caves made hiding places for fish and other sea creatures. "What about your friends?" she finally said.

"I haven't seen them either since that night. Dylan is—a jerk. Brad and Chris—well, Chris is all right, but he just goes along with them." Jeff looked down at the sand, then he laid his head back, eyes closed against the glare of the sun.

"You don't have to tell me," Marne said. "You don't have to explain."

"I want to! I feel like a—I feel terrible. All I wanted was . . . I just thought that we . . ."

"I know what you thought," Marne said drily. She stood up, brushing the sand from her legs. "Look, it's okay. I probably gave the wrong signals. Let's just forget it."

"No! No, you didn't give any wrong signals. You didn't do anything wrong. It was me. I was a jerk. I—my dad says I don't know how to treat women because I've never been around them. I'm a klutz."

She stared at him, almost starting to laugh. "You told your dad about the party?"

"Yeah. I did."

"What did he say?"

"You don't want to hear what he said. Except I told him that I wanted to talk to you and he said that was

273

appropriate, that I should apologize for putting you on the spot. So . . ." He took a deep breath. "I'm apologizing."

Marne nodded. "Okay. It's okay." She stood opposite Jeff, feeling awkward. The sand was hot under her feet. "What do you mean you haven't been around women?"

"It's not really relevant. Like, I'm not trying to make excuses."

"What did you mean?" Marne repeated, though she already knew, somehow.

Jeff rubbed the back of his neck, his profile turned to Marne as he scrutinized the sea. "Well, it's just been me and my dad. My mom left when I was nine. Didn't want to be tied down, she said. Of course, I can't blame her. My dad was working a seventy-hour week. She wanted to go back home to her people. Like we weren't her people."

"That's rough," Marne said. A dozen questions burned in her mind. She watched Jeff's face, saw his conflict, wanting to tell it and, at the same time, wanting to forget. She waited, nodding gently.

"I never saw her again," Jeff said. "She phoned twice. She sounded so—different. Like a distant relative just calling to check on things, you know?"

"Where was she?" Marne asked softly. She could imagine it, the emptiness.

274

Jeff spoke slowly, as if he were still picking up pieces of the past. "She was back in Tennessee. One time a thick envelope came. Divorce papers for my dad to sign. I guess I kept thinking she'd come back."

"I know how that is," Marne murmured. She wanted to tell him about Jody, but this wasn't the time.

"Yeah," Jeff said with a quick glance at Marne. "Well, me and my dad worked it out. He got a lady in to clean and take care of the house. He quit working so hard, spent most of every Saturday and Sunday with me. We'd go fishing and biking and stuff. It's been okay. Except I didn't have a woman to talk to, because the lady that cleaned for us hardly spoke any English, and I wasn't about to learn Portuguese. I'm not good at languages."

"You're okay with English," Marne said with a slight smile.

"But I'm not making excuses!" Jeff exclaimed. "It was my fault. I shouldn't have let those guys egg me on." He flushed and looked away again. "When I saw you jogging that first time, I was just—wow. I thought you looked great. And they were coaching me . . . telling me what to say, how to talk to you and everything."

She drew back. "Did they tell you when to kiss me?" she demanded.

275

"No. I figured that out for myself." Jeff held out his hand. She pretended not to see.

"I've got to go back and get over to the day camp," Marne said. "I promised the kids we'd make sand paintings today. We bought red and green and blue dye."

"Can I see you again?" His eyes were focused on hers.

Marne took a deep breath. *And then what?* she wondered. He stood before her, feet thrust into the sand, hands limp at his sides, looking disheveled and forlorn. Marne nodded. "Sure. Why don't you come for *Shabbos* dinner?"

"Is it okay with your aunt?"

"It will be fine."

When Marne woke up, the house was silent. It was still dark outside, but the edge of the horizon looked as if a blank page were about to unfurl, the sunlight pushing away the night. She sat up in her bed, watching the gradual transformation, aware of Becca lying in the bed beside her, aware of the sweetness of waking up and feeling attached to someone. In repose, Becca looked younger than twelve. Her cheeks were rounded and smooth, her closed eyelids glossy as a baby's. Her lips were full and deep-colored at the edges, as if they had been faintly outlined with red pencil. Jody's lips were like that, Marne remembered. She felt a swift stab of pain.

Would she ever forget the shock and the pain of Jody's disappearance? Could she attain what some people called "closure"? No. She never would. Marne could imagine herself very late in life, a grandmother perhaps, telling the story, still feeling that sharp thrust of anguish. And then, perhaps, a child's face would turn to her, the expression troubled, for children did feel things deeply, didn't they? So deeply. That child would ask her questions: "Why did it happen? How come God lets things like that happen?"

And Marne would struggle once again with the age-old question of good and evil, and depending on the age and demeanor of the child, she would answer: "Well, maybe He doesn't control people. If He did, how could we have free will? People are free to be good or bad. Unless they have that freedom, there wouldn't be any such thing as goodness, now, would there?

"It happened," she would say. "It was a random event. Why did it happen to us, when we never hurt anyone? That's what randomness is." Like a coconut falling off a tree and killing a baby; it was such a strange coincidence that it had made the front page of the paper. Chaya, drinking her morning coffee, had gasped, and the newspaper shook in her hand as she yelped, "Listen to this! Would you believe . . . oh my God! That poor mother!"

Everything had ceased. The kids still ate their cereal, but they had stopped their usual morning banter, intuitively joined to the awareness that this was big, too big for them. Jonathan looked up from spreading his bagel and asked, "Are they Jewish?"

"What difference does that make?" Chaya cried.

"I just wondered," Jonathan said, hands helplessly outspread. "I didn't mean anything . . . I would have said some extra *tehillim* for the baby today."

Marne felt her heart pound, as if she were personally involved. "You can say psalms for a non-Jew, too, can't you?"

"Of course he can," said Yitz, striding into the room. "I guess you saw the paper."

"It was the baby's time," Becca murmured, with a glance at her father. "Wasn't it?"

Yitz shrugged. He poured himself a cup of coffee from the urn on the counter. "Obviously, it was the baby's time. That doesn't mean we don't grieve. We're all connected. Something like this happens and all the relatives of that baby and all the friends of the family will suffer." He looked at Marne for a long moment. "Suffering brings us to the hardest questions about life. Why? Why do people suffer? Probably those parents are good people, too. Why?"

It was silent in the kitchen, except for the younger children slurping their cereal and Bennie banging on the tray of his high chair. The baby looked around, astonished at the silence, and to everyone's surprise he began to sing, his mouth wide open and grinning, *"Ya-da-da-da-dee . . . ,"* in clear imitation of Jonathan.

Esti clapped her hands. Yossi ran to kiss Bennie on the cheek. Chaya waited for the commotion to subside, and then she said softly, "See, that's the other side of the coin. Why don't we ask why wonderful things happen when we don't even deserve them? I never thought I could have another child after Yossi was born, and now we have Bennie. Before this summer we never even knew Marne, and now . . ." She gazed up at Marne with a slight smile and a nod. "Now . . ."

"We love her," Becca said, and she ran to link her arm in Marne's.

That night Marne told Becca about Jeff. They were lying on their beds, Marne reading her summer novel, Becca flipping through last year's camp alumni magazine.

279

Every few minutes she stopped to show Marne a photograph and to explain that child's background.

"This was one of my cabinmates, Channie. Her great-great-grandfather was a famous rabbi in Poland. Her mom teaches classes."

"Hmm," Marne murmured. "That's nice. She looks cute."

After a few minutes Becca started again. "These are the twins, Ronit and Shoshana. They've got nine brothers and sisters and about seventy cousins. Their aunts and uncles live everywhere in the world, and they can go visit for the summer. . . ."

"Becca," Marne said, "seventy cousins? All over the world? Are they all rabbis?"

"Yeah, I guess. They open *shuls,* like my parents did. Only, they had practice, because their parents all did the same thing, and they help one another. They go to conventions, and they see each other every year and talk about what they're doing to bring *Yiddishkeit,* and their kids meet at summer camp."

Marne put her book down. She turned fully to Becca. "So, when you go to summer camp, you're sort of left out, I guess."

Becca pursed her lips, nodding.

"They're all connected, somehow, old families," Marne went on. "Is that it? And your parents are . . ."

"Yeah. Kind of alone. They have friends and everything, but it isn't the same. My mom has to do everything herself. You know? She doesn't have cousins and other people to help her and give her advice."

"Your parents," Marne said, "are pioneers."

Becca looked up, astonishment in her eyes, in the wide smile on her face. "What? Pioneers? I never thought of it that way."

"Well, they are. It's easy to do something when you're just following everybody else. Your mom told me how she met your dad and they decided to be religious, even though it wasn't comfortable. It was hard, but they believed in what they were doing, and they had the guts to do it even when some people said they were nuts or . . ."

"Does your mom think we're nuts?"

"She thinks you're extreme," Marne said. "But so what? Maybe you are, maybe you aren't. It's not our business."

"What do you think?" Becca asked, staring at her.

"I think—I think you guys are really good. You try to help people. You let them be with you, and you don't try to change them. You just show them—well, alternatives."

281

Becca nodded vigorously. "That's true. Sometimes," she said, "I'm jealous."

"Of whom?"

"Of you. Is that bad?"

"Well, sometimes I'm jealous of you," Marne said, smiling. She reached out and clasped Becca's hand in her own.

Marne turned out the light, and in the darkness she began to speak, her voice low. "I saw Jeff yesterday and he told me . . ." She told Becca Jeff's story, his loss.

"Why would a mother just go and leave her son?"

"I don't know," Marne said. "It's terrible."

"Does he hate her?" Becca asked.

"No. Well, I guess he hates her and he also loves her. I feel so bad for him," Marne said. "His mother left him deliberately. She knew he'd be unhappy all his life, but she didn't care."

"She's selfish," Becca said.

"I know. Selfish. His own mother. Didn't care."

"I love you!" Becca suddenly said.

"I love you, too," Marne replied. She felt tears slipping from her eyes, covering her cheeks. She did not want to wipe away the tears, not yet. Somehow they soothed her, like a healing mist.

Into the silence Becca's voice came once more. "It's okay to cry," she said earnestly. "Mom says it's appropriate to cry when you're sad."

Marne wiped away the tears, laughing slightly. "Your mom is very smart," she said.

Gentle thoughts surrounded Marne, a parade of people passing before her, people she had met this summer. She had come to Hawaii looking for an indolent, lazy summer, with nothing but sun and sea, the sweetness of the island trade winds—a paradise summer.

Well, it wasn't like that, Marne thought. But then, how do you define paradise?

chapter TWENTY

Postcards arrived from Paris. First one, then another, then a flurry of postcards, picturing the city with its beautiful churches, broad avenues, parks, and statues.

Marne gathered them up. She sat on her bed reading them over and over until, at last, she brought them to the family room to share with the kids. They pressed close to her, Esti leaning on her lap, Elias's breath brushing her cheek, Nissim near her shoulder, and Yossi hanging over the back of the sofa. Jonathan and Becca waited for Marne to pass the cards along.

"Dear Marne, Your dad got here three days ago. My job is all done—yeah! Paris has got to be the most romantic spot on earth. This picture shows the avenue where we walked on our honeymoon so many years ago and the Arc de Triomphe. Isn't it splendid? We love you. Mom." Dad also signed the card, adding *XXOO* to his name.

Marne tried to imagine her parents walking the streets of Paris together. Would Dad's arm be around

Mom's waist? Would she look up at him with that special smile as when he surprised her with flowers or a little gift? Maybe they were holding hands. Yes, the next card went further. It was a picture of an enormous garden, beautifully tended, and the message, in a hasty scrawl: "We walk for hours every day. We met an old couple from Pasadena. They asked whether we are newlyweds! I told them we have a nearly grown daughter. Wow, next year you'll be thinking about college applications. We miss you so much. Mom and Dad. XXOO."

"We miss you . . ." She had been thinking of them together, the way they were when they first got married, without children. Without that constant tug of worries. And she'd asked herself sometimes, especially in the middle of the night, whether they would have been happier without kids. Certainly Mom had those tension moments, shown in the way she snapped a dish towel or flung pots into the sink. Kids. Damn kids! Marne could read her thoughts at those times. Now came word from Paris, "We miss you."

The next card showed the river at night, with lights reflected in the water. "Dear Marne, We want to take you here someday. Won't that be great? We haven't been spending enough vacation time together." Her dad had added, "Let's hope the stock market goes up! We're

285

thinking of going to Sweden next summer. All of us. Wish you were here. Say hi to Carole and the kids. XXOO."

And then they wrote: "Dear Marne, Please call us. Remember the time difference—twelve hours. I tried your cell, but it didn't work. It's hard for us to call you at the house, never know when you're out. We thought of having you fly here to meet us, but there's not enough time now. Love to Carole, Yitz, the kids."

Marne propped up the cards on the dresser by her bed. She telephoned Paris twice. The first time the connection was so poor, she had to hang up after just a few words, and then the circuits were busy. The next time her dad answered, sounding distant, his voice broken up. "Marne, sweetheart, this is a terrible connection. We're just going through a tunnel."

"Can you call me back?"

"We're just . . ." Static broke his voice. "Did you . . . get our cards?"

"Yes, yes. I love them. Thanks. When are you coming home?"

"We've been talking about that," her dad said. Again the connection seemed to break. "We still have to figure it out, Marne. I don't know whether they . . ." He returned and said, "Listen, we'll call you in a couple of days."

The call came on Friday.

Day camp ended early on Fridays, and Marne was washing her hair in preparation, letting it dry in the warm air while she ironed her new skirt, a delicate patchwork of pink, lavender, white, and pale blue. The full skirt came to her midcalf, and Marne liked the glamorous feel of it.

It was two in the afternoon, with several hours to go before the cleanup frenzy took hold, when the phone rang.

Jonathan answered. "Oh, Aunt Nancie Jo!"

Marne tensed, set down the iron, waiting.

"We're having a great time," Jonathan said. "Marne is teaching me guitar. She showed Becca how to make mobiles and junk sculptures. . . . Mom says she won't let her go home. Just kidding!" He turned and called, "Marne, it's your mom. From Paris."

Her mother's voice had a slightly breathless quality, a soft sound that Marne could hardly remember. "Oh, Marne, it's so beautiful here," she breathed. "This morning we walked for hours along the Champs-Élysées. We went to the top of the Eiffel Tower and then to the Left Bank, where the artists set up their easels in the street. We bought a painting. It's a Paris street scene in the rain; I know you'll love it."

"It sounds beautiful," Marne said.

"It's for you, Marne. And I got you a darling cap and a shirt and a small beaded purse. Tomorrow we're going to the Louvre and the Pompidou—fabulous art. Oh, Marne, we haven't done anything like this since . . ." There was a momentary pause, and then she went on. "Since Jody vanished. I—I guess we've been in sort of a deep freeze. I missed your dad so much. And I miss you."

"I miss you, too," Marne said, her voice heavy. "It's been a strange summer."

"Yes," her mother murmured. "A strange summer. When we're together again, we really have to talk."

"Yes."

"You took the book, didn't you?" Her voice was edged with concern. And now Marne understood that her mother had been terrified, terrified of losing her, too, so she had used silence as a shield.

"Yes," Marne said lightly, as if it didn't matter at all. "I looked at it a few times." She took a deep breath. "Last week I gave it to Nissim."

There was a great sigh. "Oh, Marne," her mother whispered. "Hey, Dad wants to say hello."

"Baby!" His tone was exuberant. "I'm trying to convince your mother to stop off in Hawaii on the way back. What do you say to that?"

Marne laughed. "I'd say your geography is lousy. Or are you circling the globe?"

"Well, I sort of thought . . . we could go surfing. Actually, I think we should. . . . It would be great to see the family. We've been so far apart."

"Oh, do it!" Marne exclaimed. "You'll love it here. You can meet all the kids and Mom and Chaya can . . ."

"Your mother's a little reluctant, you know, about getting together with her sister after all these years."

Her mother took the phone again. "Maybe she doesn't want us to come." She sounded sad, and Marne remembered all the critical remarks about Chaya and her mother's look of disdain. Or was it hurt? Hurt that Chaya had moved so far away from her former life, from her own sister?

"Nonsense," said her dad in the background. "They'd love to have us."

"I know a great condo where you can stay," Marne said. Her heart beat rapidly with excitement at the possibilities. "Kim and her family were there. They left a few days ago, I think."

"Did you have a good time with Kim?" her mother asked.

"That's something else we can talk about," Marne said. "I want you to spend some time with Becca. She's so smart and sweet." A plan had been forming in her mind for the last week or so. It would help if her parents got to know Becca. She had proposed it to Chaya just yesterday, and Chaya had sat very still for a long while, her body tense, chin resting on her folded hands.

"I'll talk to Yitz," she had said finally. "I think Becca would love it in L.A. Of course, she'd have to stay at the *yeshiva* during the week and most weekends, too. When she came to your house, there would have to be . . ."

"I know," Marne had said. "Rules. Kosher food, her own dishes or paper plates. It would be good for both of us. We'd get kosher food for her. She could come to us for *Shabbos*. I could walk with Becca to the *shul*."

"The *shul*?" Chaya gave Marne a quizzical look.

"There's one not too far from our house," Marne said. "I never paid much attention to it, but there are guys with black hats and . . ."

"Hermosa Beach," Chaya said, then let out a laugh. "Wow! I know them. I met the rabbi's wife at the convention last year. Okay. Okay. I'll talk to Yitz."

Of course, Marne hadn't mentioned it to Becca yet.

Now her mother said firmly, "Call and get us a reservation, Marne. Make it for a week from today, for three nights. Afterward, we can all fly home together."

When Marne told Chaya about the phone call, her aunt stood stock-still, and her eyes filled with tears. "She's coming here? To see us?"

"Yes. They want to be—you know, get together." Marne felt a tightness in her throat. She knew that the reunion wouldn't be smooth, and it wouldn't be easy. The two sisters would appraise each other once again, maybe still finding fault. Marne wondered, does every family have these differences? Strange relations, Marne mused. Yes, Chaya and Nance, raised as Carole and Nancie Jo, were two completely different women, but they were bound, after all, by memories and feelings that could not be denied.

Chaya stood silent, then her eyes widened and her expression grew animated. "They can stay here with us! No, I guess they'd rather be in a condo. Our house is too hectic, isn't it? But they can eat with us. Do they like gefilte fish? Kugel? Does your mother eat meat? I remember when she was going through the vegetarian phase. I did, too, nothing but tofu and cucumbers and tomatoes for nearly a year. Oh my gosh. We can go shopping. I'll show her Diamond Head at sunrise." Chaya stopped, facing Marne fully. "I've missed Nancie Jo. I didn't realize how much."

"She calls herself Nance," Marne said lightly.

Chaya laughed. "Okay, so both our names are different. Who cares? We're still family."

This time Jeff came early, bringing a basket filled with cherries. Chaya took them delightedly. "Cherries! Oh, the children will be thrilled. They have to be shipped from the mainland, so we don't usually buy them. Honestly, I don't care if I never see another pineapple or papaya for a year!"

Everything was in readiness, the table set, food prepared, the children bathed and dressed in their *Shabbos* clothes. They clamored around Jeff, wanting to play games and to show him their crafts from day camp.

"Kids! I want all of you to settle down and let Marne and Jeff . . ." She gave Marne a long look. "Marne," she said, "I almost forgot. We're all out of mustard. Would you and Jeff mind walking over to the store and getting me one of those large jars? It's an hour before candle lighting. . . . You'll make it easily."

Marne felt her face redden. She could hardly believe what she had heard. She had told Chaya about the beach party, then about Jeff's apology, and about the loss of his mother. "Are you going to tell Yitz?" she had asked fearfully.

"I don't have to go into detail," Chaya had said. "Some things are just between us. He's a nice boy. He needs a place where he can get a good meal and a taste of family life. Poor boy."

"I invited him for *Shabbos* dinner," Marne said then. "I hope that's okay."

"I was just going to suggest it," Chaya had said, grinning.

It was surprising—more than surprising—that Chaya arranged for Marne and Jeff to have time alone. Of course, it was a public street, and they were only walking together, but still, Marne wondered whether her aunt had any concerns. Her life, it seemed, was ringed by concerns, what might happen if, for instance, one small detail were omitted or done haphazardly. To Chaya it meant that the entire edifice that was Torah was in danger of crumbling. And yet, Marne had doubts. Was this true, or could there be a Judaism that leaned on tradition but still moved over into the modern world?

She had never asked such questions before. Now, she wanted to find out.

Nissim tugged at her hand. "I want to go, too. I need some fish food."

"It can wait," Marne said firmly. She bent down and gave him a quick kiss. "We're in a hurry to get back before *Shabbos,* and you take a long time deciding."

Esti and Elias were already putting on their shoes. "Let's go!"

"No," Chaya said. "You need to stay here and help me fix dessert. You can all have a taste."

Bennie toddled up to Marne, mouth open, drooling happily. He held out his arms and said, "Go bye-bye?"

Marne turned to Jeff. "Mind if we take him in his stroller?"

"Not at all," said Jeff. "He can chaperone." He nodded to Chaya. "Thanks," he said.

Somehow Marne knew this would be their last time together. There was a solemn feeling and a tenderness that comes with partings. As they walked, Marne was highly aware of every sensation—the soft fabric of the new skirt brushing her legs, the feel of the warm pavement through her sandals, the motion of Jeff's arm as he walked beside her without touching, but she noticed that their steps were in perfect synchronicity. She pushed the stroller, glad to have something to hold on to, for this time their conversation was deep and even painful.

She told him about Jody, everything, from that first encounter with the detectives to the shock and the terrible fear and guilt. "And as the years went on," she said, eyes straight ahead, pushing the stroller, "I didn't know what I wanted, what to ask for, in case asking made any difference. Did I want to find out that Jody was dead and that it was over once and for all? Did I want to find her and maybe have her reject us? And I kept asking myself, Whose fault was it? Was it my fault? Should I have been home instead of at camp? Was it my mom's fault for not locking the door? Did my father tell someone about us, someone who was a really bad person, someone he hired to fix the roof or something and he didn't bother to check him out? It went on for so long."

"Terrible," Jeff said. His face looked pinched and pale. "That's so terrible for you."

"So is your situation. Your mom leaving and everything. I guess it always seems as if other people are having a normal life, when really . . ."

"I know," Jeff said. "I kept thinking things like that. Like I was the only one with this huge problem."

"I used to think Kim's life was perfect. It does look that way, but her parents are . . . well, they just don't really pay attention to what's going on. It's all a facade."

They walked on silently for a while. Then Jeff said, "I wanted my mother to come back, and I'd imagine how I'd yell at her and tell her I never wanted to see her again, and how she'd cry for me to forgive her, but I wouldn't! I wouldn't! And then sometimes I'd have this dream that I'm just coming home from baseball practice, and she's there in the living room watching some dumb show on TV, and then I feel so great, just to see her there."

Marne nodded. They were at the store. Quickly they found the mustard and stood in line after two other people. A woman looked over at them, smiling at the baby. "Sweet-looking child," she murmured.

"My cousin," Marne said.

"Oh," said the woman, looking relieved, and Marne saw that Jeff, too, was struggling to stifle his laughter. They were so alike in some ways, like laughing when they were embarrassed or nervous, like wanting to pretend nothing really bad had ever happened to them, being haunted by it but never really talking about it.

They began the walk back, pushing the stroller together, and now there was no interruption in their conversation, no separation in their thoughts. "How can things like this happen?" Jeff said. "I mean, you'd think if you mind your own business and don't hurt anyone, things would just be normal, you know? Why'd they pick on your sister? On Jody? And why wouldn't the cops catch that person and put them in jail for life?"

"I know. It isn't fair," Marne said. "Just like it isn't fair that your mom left, and that you have to keep wondering about it and feeling bad."

"I don't feel bad. I don't really care anymore," Jeff said in a loud voice, so that Bennie turned around in the stroller and stared at Jeff.

"Bennie says you do care," Marne told him. "Look," she giggled. "He knows."

Jeff's shoulders sagged, but he was smiling. "Right. You're right. Of course I care." He moved his hands on the stroller handle, close to hers. Together they pushed the stroller up the slight incline.

Marne said, "I guess you can care about a thing and never really get over it, but then you kind of accept it. You know?"

"You have to accept it," Jeff said.

They walked on without speaking for a while. Then Jeff said, "We could keep in touch by email."

297

"Yes," said Marne. "Let's. Maybe . . . ," she began, then stopped. The world is full of maybes, she thought. Like, maybe someday she'd return to Hawaii, or Jeff would come to visit or even move back to California. There was no need, she thought, to say it.

"It's almost *Shabbos,*" Marne murmured, glancing up at the deepening sky. "Let's hurry. I have to light my candle."

They stepped up the pace. "What happens if you're late?" Jeff asked.

"What happens?" Marne smiled. "Nothing, I guess. It's just between me and God." It surprised her, talking that way to a friend, to someone outside Chaya's circle.

"So," Jeff said with a slight smile, "you and God are on speaking terms now."

Marne grinned. "Yeah. That's it. On speaking terms."

Jeff placed his hand over hers, and together they made their way back to the house.

About the Author

Sonia Levitin is the author of many critically acclaimed books of Jewish interest for young readers; among them are *Room in the Heart, The Cure,* the Journey to America series, and *Escape from Egypt*. She writes in many genres, including mystery, science fiction, and historical fiction. She is also currently at work on a musical based on her novel *The Return*.

Mrs. Levitin lives with her husband and two rescue dogs in Southern California, where she teaches university classes. Readers are invited to learn more by visiting her Web site, www.sonialevitin.com.